Man Overboard

Charles Owen

Telling Tales: Vol 3

Books by Charles Owen

Novellas:

FIAMMA

CRY CASSANDRA !

Telling Tales:

Vol 1: A CRACK IN THE GLASS

Vol 2: THE MARK OF THE BEAST

Vol 3: MAN OVERBOARD

Vol 4: ESCAPADE

Copyright

CONTENTS

Man Overboard

That morning, Karen Blake had much on her mind. The Vietnam War was coming to an end. In the United Kingdom, inflation had reached almost twenty-five per cent and the price of petrol was going through the roof. But, in a back street close to London's Piccadilly Circus, it was not those things that were occupying her thoughts.

The shiny brass plate beside the door always made her smile. It read *Kimberley Kerr, International Financial Consultants*. Roy Kerr was a one-man band. Wind and brass. But he had his uses.

Karen pushed the bell and then stood back. She lifted her chin to the camera above the doorway and showed the very tip of her tongue between a pair of full, well-formed lips. The door was opened by a young woman with shingled hair. She was wearing a tight black leather skirt and possessed the longest pair of legs that Karen had seen outside of the cabaret.

'I'll lead the way,' she said and wiggled on ahead up a narrow corridor. Karen was shown into a small bright office, simply furnished with a table and chairs and a few pictures on the walls.

'Roy – Mr Kerr, that is – will be with you in a few minutes. Shall I get you a coffee?'

Karen thanked her and when it came she swallowed it quickly. She couldn't settle. She walked around the room staring at the pictures, the violent slash and clash of colours in their shiny chrome frames, and stopped before one of them to study her reflection in the glass.

She would be twenty-eight next month. *Twenty-eight!* And God! Didn't she look every day of it! The hair was alright, straight, shoulder length, silky blonde thanks to Carlo of Knightsbridge, the genius with the bottle. But magic didn't come cheap these days. As for the tan, it looked tired and muddy, as if someone had thrown the tea slops over her.

This deal had better come off. She had forgotten what the sun looked like. She arched her neck, adjusting the gold chain at her throat. No lines there. Yet. But her eyes – the lines around them looked like the cracks in a dried-up river bed. Lord, but these last three months had been hard. If she didn't get a break soon…

She was reaching into her shoulder bag for a cigarette when the door opened. Roy Kerr was short, plump and balding. The wide stripes in his suit seemed to roller-coaster over the swollen beer gut as they struggled to follow the contours of his body.

They greeted one another. When Roy smiled, his teeth seemed to push forward like a row of old blackboard chalks squeezing up for a photograph. 'Pete looking after you alright, is he? Not keeping you up all night?' He chuckled, eating her up with his eyes.

Karen took a chair and tucked her legs under the table. 'It's time you got yourself a steady date, Roy. Think what you would save on Chinese takeaways, to say nothing of dirty movies.'

'Well, I like that,' Roy protested. 'I don't suppose I've seen one of those in a month. Anyway, what do you expect? I'm young…' He jogged vigorously on the spot, raising his knees as high as his tubby thighs allowed. 'I've got all the normal urges – cross the street and you're in Soho.' He jerked a thumb in the direction of the window. 'Out there there's still plenty of action if you know where to look for it. I live the life of a monk considering…' He subsided into a chair, blowing hard.

'And what about Fancy Pants who came to the door? She's the Mother Superior I suppose?'

'Linda? I daren't tangle with her. More than my life's worth. She's going out with a nightclub bouncer. He works in Greek Street. Built like the proverbial–'

'That's too bad.' She unzipped her shoulder bag and retrieved a leather-bound notebook. 'Now, let's hear about this man Caswell.'

Roy rolled his eyes from side to side and squeezed his lips into a dozen different shapes, like a child playing with a roll of plasticine. Then he tugged a stubby finger around the inside of his collar.

Karen arched her eyebrows sympathetically. 'Collar too tight?' She shook her head. 'That's the trouble with these cheap mail-order shirts.'

Roy leaned forward. A pen had appeared from somewhere and he jabbed it at her like a darts player preparing to throw. 'It's not my rotting shirt I want to complain about. It's my commission. For the risks I run–'

'What risks? You just–'

'*What risks!* You have to be joking! The last guy I sent you came back here in a squad car!'

Karen laughed. 'He was a right clown. We certainly turned his pockets out.'

'*Pockets!* I don't suppose the poor sod had the price of a bus fare on him. You skinned him alive. It isn't worth the–'

She raised a hand to stop the flow. '*Hang on a minute, Roy*! The law can't touch you. You put nothing in writing. You simply gave him our name. We did the rest.'

Roy raised a pudgy fist and thumped it on the table. 'You're not listening, Karen. It's not worth the aggro – not for a lousy five grand.'

'It won't happen again,' she said soothingly, keeping her voice low. 'That's a promise. These characters are all dodging the taxman or their creditors or their wife's lawyers. The last thing they want is the police involved. That's the beauty of this little…' Her eyes went to the door.

'It's alright,' Roy hissed impatiently, 'the girl's upstairs watching the monitor. One of us has to keep an eye on the street.'

'So don't worry.'

Roy thrust his chin at her. It was pink and blue, and mottled with razor rash. 'I do worry,' he growled at her. 'You want to know why?'

'Tell me.'

'Because you hit these guys so hard. Give a man a crew cut and he'll curse a bit. Probably decide that there's nothing he can do except sit on his arse till the hair grows back again. But scalp him and he's going to be so damn mad he's going to want to hurt someone.'

'Let him try.'

'That's all very well for you. You and Pete will be long gone. Toasting your fannies beside some pool on the other side of the world while muggins here–'

'Six per cent, Roy. That's top whack. And I'll still have to get the nod from Pete.'

'Seven and a half. Or I–'

'Or what? Or what, Roy?' Karen put the question very softly.

Roy ran his tongue over his lips. 'Forget I said that.'

'I already have. Pete would be very disappointed if he heard that you had been unfriendly.'

'Would I ever?' Roy spread his hands wide, the teeth jostling into place as he cranked up a smile. 'But, Karen,' he pleaded, 'do the best you can. Promise me that.'

'I'll talk to Pete.'

He rolled his lips into raw sausages and pushed a file across the table to her.

Karen flicked over the pages. 'How did you find him? Fall over him on the beach?'

Roy allowed himself a smirk of self-congratulation. 'Word gets around.'

'So I'm told.' Her fingers tapped an exasperated tattoo on the table. 'But I'm interested in where this word went walkabout. Or did Caswell find your business card pinned to his Y-fronts?'

He shrugged. 'South of Spain somewhere. I can't remember exactly. I was probably plastered at the time. One of those places with all the S's. You know – sea, sun, sand, sex, sangria – not necessarily in that order. I got an SOS from Junior. He was up the proverbial without a paddle and he'd heard that I–'

'He'd heard that you had a line to us.'

'Well, yes, he had,' Roy admitted. 'But Karen, be fair – give credit where it's due.' Resentment carried his voice higher. 'I've been in and out of every–'

'Beach bar on the Costa del Sol. Bully for you, Roy!'

'Not just the bars, Karen,' he protested, 'the clubs, *damn it,* the top restaurants, the smart hotels. When people have problems they drink too much, talk too much.'

'And the maître d' sidles up and whispers, "Go see our old buddy. Roy will give you a good steer."'

'Yeah. And sometimes I do just that. I don't shit on people all the time, Karen. If you crap in the right place, a flower comes up.'

'So what's Daffodil's problem?'

'He owes a lot of money, Karen. The thick end of a quarter of a million nicker. And his bank is getting naughty. *And I mean naughty!* He's had all the warnings. He'll have a writ by the end of the week.'

'Good timing.' She made a note on her pad. 'When did you see him?'

'On Friday. He'd just got off the plane. Shitting bricks he was.'

'What was he doing in Spain?'

'Looking for help. The place is stuffed full of people living off money they have no right to.'

'Any idiot can transfer money. The trick is to make it disappear.'

'Just what I told him. But he hasn't a clue how to set about it.'

'So he wants us to hold his hand?'

'He wasn't easy. I had to tell him the tale. Then he was climbing all over me. He wanted to see you and Pete right away.'

She shook her head. 'Let him sweat over the weekend.'

'That's what I figured.'

She turned to the file again. 'He's twenty-five. A bit of a daddy's boy, is he?'

'Daddy can't bail him out. Daddy's dead. Popped his clogs about two years ago. That's when Junior came into the money.' Roy fished in his pocket and pulled out a tube of peppermints. He blew the fluff off the top and pushed one into his mouth. 'He hadn't done much since he left university, got a degree in something weird.' He grimaced with the effort of trying to remember. 'Botany ... no, that wasn't it ... botulism...'

'Surely not!'

'Biology, that was it! At school we called it bilge. Marine Biology. He sees himself as part scientist, part explorer. He's full of fancy ideas, wants to work somewhere exciting like the South Seas or the Antarctic and eventually run his own expeditions.'

'That takes a lot of cash.'

'And he hadn't got it. He had his inheritance. He wasn't prepared to risk that. He gave himself five years to make enough money to run his own show.'

'So he went into property?'

'It was the smart move at the time. He put the word around the estate agents and within a month he had his feet behind a desk and a sign saying *Director* on the door.'

Karen turned over a page. 'Rochfort Raikes Residential? Do you know them?'

Roy sucked noisily on his peppermint. 'Did I know them?' he corrected her. 'I knew a bit about them. Quite a classy set-up. Offices in Kensington and Chelsea. They came up fast on the back of the boom. The boss was one of those flamboyant characters you get in that sort of business – knows everyone, goes everywhere ...

Ascot, Henley, Wimbledon, carnation in the buttonhole, bottle of Bolly in one hand…'

'Dolly bird in the other. I've got the picture.' She frowned. 'But why did they want Caswell unless they needed some mug to put money into the business?'

Roy grinned, 'Good try. They were expanding rapidly. They needed more working capital so they went to the bank for a big loan. Caswell was promised–'

'Let me guess. A directorship? Right away if he guaranteed the loan.'

'You got it. The market was on the slippery slope but Junior didn't twig. He was told that the business was making pots of money, the bank guarantee was just a formality and would be dispensed with inside a year. By that time, his biggest problem would be finding ways of spending his salary.'

Karen made a note in the file. 'When the cabin boy suddenly gets promoted to the bridge,' she murmured, 'the rest of the ship's company are usually in the lifeboat.'

'And lowering away. That was the score. The other directors buggered off, the business went belly up and Caswell was left looking at the pieces.'

'So, our friend owes a quarter of a million pounds and the bank have put the bite on him. Can he raise it?'

'Just about. But it would clean him out. Karen, don't you think–'

'I think we are trying to run a business, Roy. Where's Caswell's money at the moment?'

'He'd got it put aside to buy a house in London. Then he was going to get himself a cottage down on the south coast and a sail boat.'

'So the money is on deposit?'

'That's what he told me.'

'Better and better.' She turned to the last page in the file. 'He's got no job. He owes all this money. How can he afford to live in a house in Chelsea?'

'He's just caretaking for a few days for a friend of his. The guy's away on a business trip.'

Karen pushed back her chair and stretched her legs. 'What does Caswell use for brains?'

Roy screwed up his eyes. He liked people to know that he was thinking. 'Caswell's not a plonker, I'll say that for him. He'll turn up with a cheque book and if you and Pete do your stuff, he'll sign. Most of these berks need a lawyer on one side and an accountant on the other just to hold their pants up.'

'How much did you tell him about Pete and me? About the set-up?'

'I gave him the usual bull.'

'What you're trying to say,' said Karen severely, 'is that you briefed him as we agreed. Did you tell him that Pete was a highly successful investment adviser who works for a small number of very rich confidential clients – people who need to operate in complete secrecy?'

'And that you are a lawyer and an expert on offshore tax,' Roy recited wearily. 'I tell you – I gave him the whole spiel – how you had houses all over the world – an apartment on Fifth Avenue, a house in Paris, a chalet in Zermatt, a penthouse in Eaton Square–'

'The penthouse at least is true – for the next few days at any rate. You told him we were married?'

'Of course. We agreed we'd keep things simple.'

Karen sighed. 'If only they were.'

'Why doesn't Pete marry you? *The tight-fisted git!'*

'Now then, Roy! Pete wouldn't like to hear you talking about him like that.' She chewed at a knuckle. 'But he can be very difficult.'

'Difficult!' Roy snorted. 'He's bloody impossible. What's he waiting for? He must have tucked away a small fortune these past few weeks.'

Karen hunched her shoulders, massaging the back of her neck. 'Money doesn't solve everything. He doesn't need me as much as–'

'*Doesn't need you!* He couldn't work this without you – or me for that matter. We catch his chickens for him. When he gets them, they're oven-ready. All he has to do is turn the heat up.'

She rose to her feet. 'You only see part of the picture. We've been together for over seven years. When we met he'd taken a very cold bath – lost all the money he'd made over ten years. Now he's just about back where he was then.

'But it's been a bumpy ride. Always on the move, keeping one step ahead of the law, always watching your back, never sure when you walk into a hotel, a restaurant or an airline office that somebody you never wanted to see again hasn't recognised you and picked up the telephone. Passports, bank accounts, hotel bookings, all in false names, bogus photographs. Pete has changed his appearance so often I've forgotten which version is the real one.' She laughed humourlessly. 'Perhaps there never was a real one.'

Roy walked with Karen to the door. 'You sound as if you could do with a holiday. When are you and Pete moving on?'

'Friday night, if we can put this deal to bed by then.'

'And if you can't?'

'Friday night, just the same. We've been in London almost a month and that's a long time in our business. It gets to you after a bit. You get the runs every time you hear a police siren.'

'You needn't tell me.'

Karen put a hand on his arm. 'Don't worry about your commission, Roy, I'll square Pete. And if Mr Caswell desires a consultation…'

Roy drew himself up to a pudgy five and a half feet. 'Mr Caswell most sincerely desires a consultation…'

'Then ask him if he'd like to have lunch with us tomorrow. Twelve noon at Eaton Square. But to come in comfortable clothes. Karen and Pete are very informal. You know the line to take. Tell him that Pete doesn't normally handle these small sums, but to–'

'To oblige a friend of a friend…'

'Exactly. And ask him to make sure he's got instant access to his account – and to bring his cheque book.'

'He could bring cash.'

Karen shook her head. 'No. You can't withdraw that sort of money without making special arrangements. And that would frighten him. He'll cry off if we suggest it.' She tucked the folder into her bag.

Roy offered a plump white hand. It was warm and damp. 'No point in asking for your forwarding address?'

'None. I'll give you a call before we go and let you know how things went.'

'I'll be waiting for it – and for my whack.'

Karen nodded. 'Say goodbye to Linda for me.'

The door closed quickly behind her. She walked to her car, a dark-blue BMW. It looked right and people noticed these things. It would be a wrench giving it back. She drove quietly, keeping one eye on the mirror. That got to be a habit after a time.

She would have a look at the offices where James Caswell had worked, drive past the house where he was staying. Pete was bound to check. He liked to get a feel for a new client before a meeting – and he was merciless on sloppy homework. The last time he had lost his temper with her he had left her so bruised it was a week before she could show her face outside.

2

From his chair behind a huge mahogany partners' desk,
Peter Vance looked over a small battery of telephones
to banks of screens and keyboards, telexes spewing
their endless tongues of white tape and chattering fax
machines. He rose as Karen opened the door and they
walked together into the drawing room and stood a little
back from the windows. It was Tuesday and shortly
after noon.

'All systems go?'

'Yes, Pete. All systems go.'

They looked over the tops of trees in full green leaf
to an acre of elegant roofs and heavy grey slates that
kept the rain off some of the richest people in the world.
A pigeon swooped in the warm air.

Vance was a large man. As he turned back towards
the room, the space around him seemed to shrink. The
massive head would have held its own in a hall at the
British Museum devoted to Egyptian temple carvings.
When he walked, his hands seemed to lead his body as
if thrusting his way through a crowd.

He dressed carefully. The crisp linen suit in dark
midnight-blue had the stamp of Savile Row about it, the
lemon silk shirt with the discreet monogram on the
pocket that of Jermyn Street. In fact, both had been
purchased in a back alley in Hong Kong at a fraction of
London prices. A close observer might have remarked
that for a man of his bulk, the feet shod in glossy
Ferragamo shoes were surprisingly small.

A buzzer sounded in the hall outside. A
manservant, immaculately attired in starched white

cotton jacket and black trousers hovered in the doorway. 'Your guest has arrived, Sir.'

'What name did he give?' Vance asked sharply.

'Mr Caswell, Sir,' the servant replied, a hint of reproach in his voice.

'Very well, Bruford. Show Mr Caswell in.'

Vance and Karen stood like royalty in the middle of the drawing room while James Caswell walked rather diffidently through a snowdrift of white carpet to greet his hosts. Vance stepped forward, smiling broadly. 'I'm Peter. This is my other half, Karen. Call me Pete – everybody does.'

'It's good of you to see me at such short notice.'

'Not at all. Glad if we can be of help. Karen, find James somewhere to perch while I rustle up a drink.'

Some perch, Caswell thought as he seated himself at the end of a long double-sofa upholstered in glistening ivory leather. He held himself rather stiffly, resting his hands on his knees and gazed around him. There were large picture windows running the length of the room framed by silk curtains in shimmering gold. The walls, dressed in white kid, set off the enigmatic Magritte prints. On a table in the centre, a fountain of tall arum lilies rose from an elegant delft vase. A clock of the Second Empire dominated the marble mantelpiece and in the alcoves to either side stood heavy bronze busts of Wellington and Napoleon.

'What a magnificent apartment,' he said at last. 'It quite takes my breath away.'

Karen smiled at him. 'We like it,' she said casually. 'It's comfortable and easy to run. We have its twin on the other side of the hall, which is such a help.

We are away travelling a great deal and the staff have somewhere to stay and can keep an eye on things.'

Caswell's mouth fell open. 'You mean that you run another apartment like this for the staff?'

Vance laughed. 'Not quite like this – we can't afford to buy them lilies.' He lifted a bottle of champagne from a silver ice bucket. 'Roederer alright for you, James?' He eased out the cork and poured the foaming liquid into three tall flutes.

'Fine. Thank you. Yes,' Caswell stammered, 'if it isn't too much trouble?'

'No trouble at all, James. It wants drinking and what better time than the present?' He raised his glass to his guest. 'Here's to a speedy resolution of the little difficulties we've been hearing about.' For a fraction of a second his pale eyes held Karen's over the rim.

'I'll drink to that,' Caswell agreed fervently, gulping at his drink before setting down the glass heavily on the onyx table before him.

Vance rubbed his chin and smiled behind his fingers. He wasn't one to count his chickens prematurely but this operation looked as if it would be easy. Caswell was in a blue funk. His nerves were strung tight. It showed in his speech, in the stiffness of his posture, in his over-deferential manner. With his clean-cut features, black hair neatly combed and parted, and dark, anxious eyes, he was good-looking, even very good-looking in an unfledged way. The starched white collar and the grey flannel suit reinforced the boyish impression. A newly appointed prefect taking a glass of sherry with the headmaster.

Caswell's eyes kept coming back to Karen. Vance surmised that the youth had in all probability never in his life set eyes on such a creature. Her trouser suit was cut very close. Too close. He would have a word with her later. There was business to be done and a line should be drawn between attraction and distraction. He caught her eye and tilted his head a degree or so in the direction of the dining room.

Karen stood up and with a mutinous finger trailed a wisp of golden hair behind her ear. 'I will go and bully the chef and find out how lunch is getting on. Pete will give you a conducted tour, James. I know he's just dying to show you his toys.' She walked away from them with a long stride and an easy, rhythmic swing of her hips.

Vance turned away quickly and recharged their glasses. 'Would you like to see where the work is done, James?' He waved a hand at the room. 'And see what pays for all this?'

'Very much.' Caswell dragged his eyes back from the retreating figure and followed Vance to an arch in the corner where a heavy, soundproofed door led to the adjoining room. This was cool and brightly lit. Behind the desk, a whole wall was taken up by a large relief map. Banks of screens ran in a horseshoe round the room.

Vance pointed at the map. 'Watch very closely and you can see the areas of light and darkness changing all the time. In London it is just after midday, but in Japan the moon is coming up over Tokyo Bay. But night or day, there's constant, relentless activity. The global market never sleeps.'

'Very impressive,' Caswell remarked. 'I don't suppose there are too many offices like this in Belgravia.'

'I doubt if there's another dealing room like this in Europe.' He arched a pair of sandy eyebrows as if inviting dissent. 'You think that's just sales patter. Pete giving you the pitch?'

'No – not if you say so...'

Vance put his arm around Caswell's shoulder. 'Take nothing on trust, old son. If I make a claim for what I can do, make me prove it. Be satisfied with nothing less. I like you, James. We are going to be buddies, you and I. And Karen will tell you, I'll do anything to get a friend out of a hole. But make no allowances on that account. Business is business. Do we understand each other?'

'Yes, indeed. I'm most grateful to you for being so frank.'

Vance nodded. He pointed to the long line of screens. 'Come and take a look. I think it will interest you. All the important numbers are there. Share and commodity prices, options, futures, derivatives, barter trades, currency movements, money volumes flowing across the exchanges. You can see hotel occupancy figures, passenger loadings on international business flights, container ship manifests – all pointers to where the action is, who's on top and who's going down the pan.'

'It's astonishing!'

Vance shrugged. 'It's routine. Without it you don't get to first base. We need a lot more than that to stay in front. We have other, less orthodox sources. Some of the information is in our hands before it reaches the government trade ministers. Some of it is highly classified.'

'Isn't that–'

'Illegal?' Vance turned to look at the questioner, his eyes moving over Caswell's face like an archaeologist working over a new site, passing swiftly over areas which would yield him nothing but probing carefully, patiently where examination would bring its reward.

'I won't duck that question – or any other. In a tough world, we have to be competitive to earn a living. If we are going to be successful, we need an edge. A plane which flies faster. A gun which fires further. Information is my business. And who has the edge in the information business? *Government!'*

He paused for a moment but his mouth was still at work as though the machinations of an overactive brain demanded an outlet. 'Why,' he continued, 'do you suppose that companies are prepared to pay enormous salaries to obtain the services of ministers who have held key government posts? Because it is the only way that they can put their hands on information which is denied to them.'

As Vance's argument developed, the powerful hands came into play, assembling, building, giving shape to the obstacles in his path, then flattening them one after the other, sweeping the debris aside, pushing forward once more. 'Forget the aristocracy. Forget the big landowners. Their time has come and gone. Politicians and bureaucrats are the new ruling class. Can I beat that lot fair and square? *Of course not!* It can't be done. So I have to cut a few corners.'

They were back at the top of the room. Vance leaned over his desk and tapped in a series of numbers on the board. 'See that!' He read off the screen, *'Supertanker Globestar, twelve hours sailing out of the*

Persian Gulf, 250,000 tons of crude, destination Genoa. In the time it takes you to walk around this room, James, I could buy that cargo. If the numbers stacked up, I could sell it at Aden, buy it back before it was in the Med or turn it round and send it to Tokyo.'

'Using your own money?' Caswell asked doubtfully.

'I may be a rich man,' Vance chuckled, 'but not that rich. No, I'd buy it for a client, or a small syndicate and take a share myself. My clients give me total discretion. They pay me to make money – not excuses. They don't want to know about tax or inflation or risk. All they want to hear is that they are richer today than they were yesterday.'

'I doubt whether the money I have is enough to interest you,' said Caswell disconsolately. 'Two hundred and fifty thousand pounds is a lot to me but...' He came to an embarrassed silence. Vance pursed his lips. 'It is a smallish parcel for us,' he admitted. 'We would normally charge fifteen per cent commission on that sort of deal.' Then, seeing Caswell flinch, he added, 'But we would give you a special price – a *prix d'ami*. We would work on ten. After paying our agent, there wouldn't be a date stone in it for us but today's grateful client is tomorrow's valuable customer.'

'It still seems rather steep. Twenty-five thousand pounds for making a transfer which–'

'Which we can set up in a few minutes. In the ordinary way I would agree, but this is not a straightforward deal. We are not merely moving your assets from one place to another, James. We are placing them beyond the reach of your creditors and we are covering your tracks.'

He splayed a large hand and counted off on his fingers. '*First*, we need a country where the anonymity of depositors is inviolate and reinforced by penal sanctions under banking law. *Second*, it must be a tax shelter. There's no fun in seeing your dividends paid away to fund a dog toilet in Battersea Park. *Third*, the money must be placed in a bank where the management is efficient and, above all, discreet. *Finally*, we need to set up a secret numbered account for you.

'All this calls for considerable expertise. Expertise doesn't come quick and it doesn't come cheap. That's what you are paying for.' He smiled. 'And our job doesn't stop there. We don't run away. We are still here making sure that all the sandbags are in place when the water starts rising.'

Caswell passed a hand over his forehead. 'I'm sorry ... I don't quite follow...'

Vance groaned inwardly. *Lord*! They didn't come much thicker than this fellow! '*Right*! We will take this slowly. You were a partner in a firm of estate agents and you guaranteed a loan from the bank. The business folded. Unsurprisingly, the bank wants its money back. You haven't paid and a writ from the bank is imminent. Is that the position?'

'It is.'

'Very well. Then you must move fast. Banks work closely together. The day that writ arrives, you may find that your own bank account has been frozen.'

'Is that possible?' Caswell asked in some agitation.

'Very possible. The banks are no slouches when they get the wind up. You must shift that cash at once.'

'And when the writ arrives...'

'You won't be able to defend it. You owe the money. But relax, old son, the money has gone. All that lovely lolly you had sitting on deposit has disappeared – whisked away from under the bank's nose. But where has it gone? The bank will ask you a lot of awkward questions. They won't believe that you lit the fire with it by mistake, that it fell down a manhole or that you lost it at the races. They will threaten to make you bankrupt – and that can be very tiresome.'

'I realise that now.' Caswell was very subdued. 'I hadn't really thought it through. I imagined ... I hoped that my problems were really over as soon as the money was out of the country.'

Vance spread his hands wide. '*Your* problems are over the moment you instruct us to make the transfer. Leave us to do the worrying. That's what we're paid for. You go and have a nice holiday and come back when things have quietened down.'

He turned to the map on the wall. 'Where would you like to visit your money, James? How about the *Caymans*?' A red bulb lit up showing the exact location of the islands.

'How did you make that happen? It's extraordinary! I swear I didn't see–'

Vance laughed. '*Voice recognition*! Like a well-trained Welsh collie, it comes when you call. Today it seems like magic. Tomorrow it will be commonplace.' He raised his glass and drained it, wiping his mouth with the back of his hand. 'Personally, I don't like islands. I find them rather cramping. You can walk across Grand Cayman in under an hour. Boring you might say, but they have a helluva lot of banks. Some five hundred. And there are thirty thousand registered companies and probably as many crocodiles, not all of them living in the swamps. You've got to know your way around. Go into some of those places and you'll be counting your fingers on the way out to see how many you've got left.'

He pitched his voice a tone higher. 'Or you might like *Bermuda* ...' another red bulb blinked back at them, 'where the drinks are long and the shorts are short ... or *Liechtenstein.* I remember driving there in a Ferrari. It's so tiny you can miss it between gear changes. Or you may prefer *Monaco*, which comes complete with a prince and a palace straight out of Gilbert and Sullivan. Believe me, James, there are few things better than sprawling in a deckchair watching the sun sparkling off the bluest water you've ever seen, with a bird on one side and a glass of ice-cold Krug on the other, thinking of all the poor sods back home going to work crammed into the Tube like sardines in a can.'

Caswell smiled. 'I think I could get to like Monte Carlo.' Then, more soberly, 'But one has to live somewhere, Pete, and the hotels are expensive.'

'Very true,' Vance conceded. 'But a good-looking young man, someone like you, with your brains, can always make out. I knew a guy, one of our clients, who went out to Monte. His circumstances were very like your own. Within a week he was living with a rich American woman, a divorcée who wrote social chit-chat for the glossy magazines. I believe it worked very well. He fed her with the local gossip and kept the bloom on her cheeks and she paid the bills. For all I know, he's still there.'

'I confess I am warming to the idea.' Caswell's eyes were bright and he spoke with mounting enthusiasm. 'Suppose,' he went on more cautiously, 'suppose I agree to your terms. What guarantee do I have that ... that…'

'That the money will actually arrive?' Vance was amused.

'Well, yes...' Caswell blurted out, his face reddening. 'Pete, please don't think that I don't trust you... It's just that this is a big step for me and I can't afford to make a mistake. You do understand?' he concluded, on a note of appeal.

Vance tapped the side of his nose with a broad finger. 'You're a cautious man, James, I like that. There is an old salesman's adage. "If someone throws business at you," – he inclined his head sharply – ' *"Duck!"* Why? Because it will be bad business. You're right not to be rushed into a deal. Trust is built slowly – one step at a time.'

'But you said–'

'That you must move quickly, James. *Quickly but carefully*.' He pushed back a starched white cuff and glanced at his watch. 'Now, this is what I propose. Today is Tuesday. If I have your cheque in my hands today, it will be cleared by midday on Friday. If you want your cash in Monte – and we'll look at the tax angles with Karen – it will be in your numbered account before the banks close for business that same day. Is that quick enough for you?'

Caswell nodded. 'Friday will be fine.'

'Excellent. By five o'clock that afternoon you will receive a call from the manager. He will ask you to confirm your name and give his own. He will then request that you telephone him as soon as possible. You should return his call from a public telephone box. The number you dial is a direct line so you will get straight through. You will know the name of the bank because I shall give it to you but you must not mention it during your call.

'The manager will confirm the balance standing to your credit and will advise placing it on deposit in a rock-solid currency. Agree to what he suggests. He will not give you the number of your account and you should not ask for it. Make an appointment to visit him as soon as convenient. When you meet, he will be able to answer any questions that you have and to advise on investing the money. Have I made myself clear?'

'Perfectly.'

'Good. Follow the procedure for your protection – and for ours.' His fingers tapped silently on the desk top. 'I can see that something else is troubling you...'

Caswell frowned. 'If I give you my cheque today and the money is banked on Friday, there are three days–'

'Three days during which you are out of your money. And that, quite understandably, causes you a little anxiety.' He took a cheque book from an inside pocket, laid it on the desk and took out a gold fountain pen.

Caswell stared at the pen. It was a gold Dunhill and not plated. He could see the hallmark engraved on the jacket. Probably eighteen carat. Two thousand pounds worth if it was a penny.

Seemingly oblivious of the impression he had made, Vance recited as he wrote. 'To James Caswell pay the sum of two hundred and fifty thousand pounds.' He signed the cheque, dated it and handed it to Caswell. 'When your money is in your account, please destroy this.' Then he picked up the telephone and dialled a number. 'No doubt you know of my bank, James?'

Caswell, an expression of awe on his face, was looking at the cheque in his hand. 'Yes ... yes, I do.' Its name was rarely out of the financial press, a small, lively merchant bank on the fringe of the City.

Vance nodded. He raised the mouthpiece. 'Peter Vance here, may I have a quick word with the General Manager?' A few moments later, he said, 'Harold Quinton? Good afternoon. You recognise my voice? Splendid! It's inimitable you say? Well, you must blame a misspent youth in the Cape for that. Now, Harold, you're a busy man and I'm pressed for time myself so I'll come straight to the point.

'I have at my side a Mr James Caswell with whom I hope to transact a little business. Mr Caswell is holding my cheque for two hundred and fifty thousand pounds as security until our business is concluded. He is far too polite to ask whether I have two hundred and fifty thousand pounds ... you find that entertaining, Harold, but then you have the advantage of my charming friend. Allow me to pass you over to him and be so good as to tell him how that account stands. Many thanks – we'll be in touch later.' He handed the receiver to Caswell and engrossed himself in one of the commodity screens, returning when the conversation had ended.

'Over two million pounds...' Caswell confirmed, his voice low and reverential.

Vance airily waved a hand. 'It's often much more.' He propped himself on the edge of his desk while Caswell produced his own cheque book. Vance's expression was relaxed, casual yet attentive, the attitude of an older man, wise in the ways of the world, placing himself at the disposal of a friend in need of good counsel.

His hands rested easily upon his lap but a tremor ran through his fingers. The arduous stalk was approaching its climax, the hunter watching his prey moving into the line of his sights, every nerve disciplined as, infinitely gently, he takes up the pressure on the trigger. 'If there is anything else, James, on which you have any misgivings ... you have only to ask.'

'I hesitate to suggest it, but there is one last thing…'

Vance exhaled a long, silent breath. 'You have only to say–'

'It would be reassuring to have a brief note from you on your headed paper, if that isn't too much to ask. Just a few lines confirming that you hold my cheque and will make the transfer on Friday as we arranged.'

Vance considered this for a long moment. Then he slapped the leather top of the table and stood up. 'You drive a hard bargain, James, but I agree.' He held up a hand. 'I must, however, impose a condition. That letter is for your eyes only. The moment your money has arrived, you must destroy it. You can see that it could be very damaging if it ended up in court.'

'How could that happen if you do what you promise?'

Vance blinked quickly. 'It might fall into the wrong hands. It could be used to put pressure on us.'

'I understand. You have my word on it.'

'Splendid.' Vance picked up a microphone, pressed a button and dictated. He turned to Caswell when he had finished. 'Before you leave us this afternoon, you shall have your letter.'

Caswell wrote out his cheque, passed it to Vance and they shook hands.

'Now let's go and eat,' Vance suggested. 'We've worked hard and can enjoy our lunch with a good conscience.'

Karen looked up as the two men came through the door. 'I hope you have brought your appetites with you. I'm starving.'

'I am hungry, I must confess.' For the first time, Caswell spoke with real animation. His step was lighter and more confident as if a mountain of care had been lifted from him.

Vance, a step or so behind his guest, tapped his breast pocket in a sign to Karen. Things were going according to plan. The small party proceeded to the dining room.

'We're using the small dining room today,' Karen explained. 'It's more friendly when we are just a few. The big one is like something out of Versailles.'

Bruford padded soundlessly around the table replenishing their glasses.

'It's a Montrachet,' said Vance, 'and drinking very well this year.' Karen smiled a little sadly. Pete had no problem thinking himself into the part. He revelled in it, sloughing the old skin for a shiny new one, slipping into it like the self he might have been had things gone differently. Dreamily she watched the sunlight with its mocking dance leaping back and forth among the silver and the crystal, running to her only when she turned her head, scattering its coins about her like a waterfall.

If Caswell was expecting to say more about himself, his host spared him the trouble. What little curiosity Vance had on the subject seemed to have been satisfied by his lieutenants. He was a man who enjoyed holding centre stage.

'The people I deal with, the super-rich, live in constant dread of being beggared. It puzzled me for a long time and then I hit upon the answer. How can they believe in possessions acquired with so little effort? The mismatch between the rewards of successful speculation and the exertion involved is grotesque.' He reduced a bread roll to crumbs beneath his fingers. 'They need reassurance – almost hour by hour – that their colossal wealth is not merely an illusion, a mirage – which, at the blink of an eye, may vanish and leave them paupers.'

'Yes, I can see that,' Caswell replied mechanically. He was only half-listening, saving one eye for his host while watching Karen's fingers running up and down the stem of her glass. Now she was drawing a succulent asparagus spear into her mouth, softly pressing the juicy membrane between her lips, the pale gold of her cheeks hollowing as she drew the essence from it, then with exquisite delicacy, chasing a glistening film of butter with the tip of her tongue.

'I suppose it is a penalty of success. I'm on call twenty-four hours a day. It's worse than being a doctor. A client can telephone at three o'clock in the morning – he can't sleep and wants to talk to Uncle Pete. Nobody else will do. There's a report that a minister in South America has been assassinated or there's news of an earthquake in Japan or a hurricane in the Gulf of Mexico, and he's panicking and nothing less than a promise to send him a printout of all his holdings – instantly – will get him off the line.'

Karen winked at Caswell. 'The old and neurotic curl up at night with their insomnia, the young–'

'Karen, please,' Vance remonstrated, 'not now.'

'Well, they're a miserable lot!'

'I don't disagree but they happen to be our living. As for neurotic, you're right. They are just like the old miser who is woken by a noise in the middle of the night.' Vance's eyes dilated, showing a lot of white and he cupped a hand to his ear. *'What was that?'* He sat bolt upright in his chair. 'The old man wakes with a start, a cold sweat breaking on his forehead. At that very moment, a thief may be creeping into his house to sneak off with his treasure!'

Karen rolled her eyes at Caswell as if to say, just look at the old ham, he's well away now.

Vance put a trembling hand to his throat. 'Clutching his gown about him, he takes his lantern and creeps downstairs.' He lowered his voice to a whisper and his head seemed to sink between his shoulders like a giant turtle retreating into its shell. 'Down the steps to the cellar where the air is dank and musty and the ceiling dripping with moisture. The shadows seem to arch over him like assassins poised to strike! In terror he raises the lantern and the shadows draw back, flattening themselves against the walls!

'He crouches down over the hiding place, lifts up the stone, scrabbles with his nails like a dog at the hard-packed earth beneath. *He can feel the bag!* Tearing open the neck, he thrusts his hands deep into the metal, scooping it up by the handful, letting it trickle through his fingers. Now he must try a coin between his teeth, feel its temper, its virtue, its readiness to shield him from want and sickness and old age. Still it is not enough, he must reach deep down, like a midwife into the womb of the earth, bring forth his little store of happiness, hug its burgeoning life to his body like a mother nursing her baby, envelop it, feel it growing warm, becoming one with him.'

'Oh, come now, Pete,' Karen protested, 'you are getting carried away. What do you know about women nursing babies?' And then, disconcerted at the edge her voice had found, she called to Bruford to clear away the plates.

Vance made no answer. He stared at Karen, his mouth working soundlessly.

Caswell plunged awkwardly into the uncomfortable silence. 'How did you get started, Pete? Was your father a businessman?' Karen brought her hands softly together in appreciation.

Vance glanced from one to the other before beginning tentatively. 'Karen will have to bear with me – she's heard this many times before. I was raised in South Africa. I never got to know my father. He pushed off when I was eight. The old man worked in the meat-packing business. When he came home in the evening, so tired sometimes that he could hardly get upstairs, my mother used to run behind him with a spray – she complained that he made the house smell like a stockyard.'

'Pete, you're exaggerating. You always–'

'*No, Karen! It's the gospel truth*! She ran behind him spraying eau de cologne!' He turned to Caswell. 'My mother was French. She always thought that she had married beneath her.' He snapped off a lobster claw and drove a pick like a burglar's jemmy into the shell and prised it open. 'Extracting a kind word from that woman was like finding a shred of nourishment in this bloody thing.'

Karen made a face at Caswell. 'Now you know why Pete hates women.' She spoke lightly but her eyes, resting on Caswell's for a moment, were sombre.

'That's nonsense, Karen. I don't hate women. I'm not prepared to have them take over my life – that's all.' He smiled at Caswell. 'You mustn't mind the way we carry on, James. Karen and I are a pair of lovebirds but like all happily married couples, we can't resist taking the odd peck at one another.'

'You were going to tell James...' Karen prompted.

'How I got started?' Vance helped himself to the lemon soufflé. 'I left school at sixteen – smartest move I ever made – and went to work for a mining company. They must have taken a shine to me because they sent me to Europe, to a business school in France. I had just turned twenty. It was a tough year and being half an hour's drive from Paris with all its temptations didn't make it any easier. Most of the tuition was in French and German and they drove us like galley slaves. We forgot whether it was day or night, winter or summer. We just worked.'

Karen closed her eyes, feeling the warmth of the sun on her face. Pete was well into his stride now. She had heard the story so many times before, the strands of fact and fantasy braided so tightly together, she wondered that he or she could still tell one from the other.

'Most of the stuff they taught us was rubbish. Academics know the theory of running a company but they can't teach you how to build a great business. They don't understand that to do that you need an exceptional man, one in a million, the guy with the X Factor. He's worth more than all their algebraic formulas put together.'

Karen sighed softly. Nobody told the whole truth about themselves. People talked in a sort of Morse code, emitting dots and dashes of light, leaving one to puzzle out the darkness in between. After a term at the school, Pete had flunked out, gone to live with a rich Parisienne off Saint-Germain-des-Prés. There was some Jewish blood and she had family connections in banking in Frankfurt and New York. Pete was a good-looking young man, little more than half her age. She was a widow with plenty of money, time on her hands and amused to further the career of her protégé. They became lovers, used each other and when there was nothing left, parted, apparently without rancour.

'I ditched the mining company and went into investment banking.'

More likely the company had ditched him – cut their losses. Karen wasn't sure. Even after seven years there was much that she didn't know about him, might never know. Pete had this curiously naïve view of human nature, priding himself that he could read character the way a good accountant could read a balance sheet. He was fond of claiming that, 'If I could buy that fellow at my valuation and sell him at his own, I would make a very nice profit.' But he was always astonished when others weighed him up, did the same calculation and reached the same answer.

Pete had the brains and the energy to get to the top of the mountain but he despised the conventional route, the life-sapping effort of climbing, the politicking, the in-fighting to maintain his place on the ascent, the toadying to men above him, men whom he saw as his natural inferiors. He was always looking for that magical short cut. It had to be there. Nature made exceptions for creatures like him. He should soar effortlessly to the summit, alight like an eagle – not crawl every inch of the way like a centipede.

'That took me to Germany and the US and then to Tokyo. The money was good but there were better opportunities in oil trading.'

Blockade-running. That was the real name for it. Buying up cheap oil blocked under UN embargo, piping it overland to a sanction-free port for re-export. The risks were huge and so were the profits. Pete could have taken his share and gone straight, had a stab at becoming a respectable citizen, married her, had a few kids. But it was never the right time to quit. One more deal, Karen, and then we'll call it a day. Garage our winnings and put our feet up. Who knows, I might even make an honest woman of you.

Caswell had relaxed, opened his jacket and loosened his tie. He sipped at his glass, rolling the Sauternes over his tongue. 'Tell me, Pete, how did you and Karen meet up?'

Vance flashed a warning to Karen. This was dangerous ground.

'Wasn't it at the airport...?' She kept her eyes on him, staying close to the prompter like an actress uncertain of her lines.

Vance tapped his forehead as if the recollection had only at that moment come to him. 'You're right. I believe it was ... yes, I'm sure it was Schipol.' He grinned at Caswell. 'I arrived at the airport in a taxi. The rain was teeming down and there was this long queue of people waiting for a cab to take them into Amsterdam – and poor bedraggled Karen stuck at the end of it. I thought she was the most beautiful woman I had ever set eyes on. I still do, for that matter.'

Karen blew a kiss at him. 'Pete, that was a very nice little speech.'

Vance took her hand and kissed the tips of her fingers. He turned to Caswell. 'I told the driver to pick her up and find out where she wanted to go. You can imagine what he said to me. There were fifty people ahead of Karen, standing there with the water running down the backs of their necks, and by that time most of them were looking our way. The cabbie was afraid of being lynched and I can't say I blame him.'

Karen laughed and took up the story. 'Pete can be quite persuasive when he makes up his mind that he wants something. Anyway, I jumped in and we drove off. All those disappointed punters were shouting at us.'

'And banging on the windows,' Vance continued. *'Lord! It was funny!'*

'It was a crazy day, James. If you could have seen us…'

'Karen had just flown in from Indonesia. She had a job with an American law firm. The money was good but she was going nowhere. And I was tired of working for other people and had decided to go solo. It took two laps of the airport before she agreed to join forces and come to Bahrain with me.'

It wasn't quite like that. Bruford arriving with the cigar box broke in on Karen's reflections. Pete would spend the next few minutes telling James how he bought the world's finest Cuban cigars in Dubai at half price.

'Hoyo de Monterrey, James. You should try one. The Number 1 in my view is unsurpassed. Do you know what I pay for these?'

She had met Pete at Schipol Airport – or, rather, Pete needed to meet someone fast and he had found her. Interpol was close on his heels and he was afraid he wouldn't get through passport control. He had got into bad company in Australia. It should have been a nice little scam. He and his cronies had bought a few square miles of dirt in the back of beyond, flown in a couple of crooked surveyors, a so-called geological survey team, and filed an optimistic preliminary report. The rumour industry and the share-pushers did the rest. They never put a spade in the ground.

Then things went wrong. Pete flew to Holland to pick up his cut but the police had got there first. Those who hadn't been put in the slammer had scarpered and taken the money with them. He could have driven across the frontier or taken a train but he had a deal brewing in Jordan and he was in a hurry. It was typical of him to up the stakes and try to take a flight out.

His best hope was that the official at the desk, a Himmlerite figure with a long, thin, sallow face and wire-rimmed spectacles, would be looking out for a man travelling alone and wouldn't spot the false passport.

'Do you remember that frightful lipstick I was wearing, Pete? Bright scarlet – and when I kissed you it left those ghastly smears?'

'How could I forget?' Vance held the cigar to his nose, crackling the leaf between his fingers.

How indeed. It is very difficult to take a close look at a man's face while his companion is making a great play with a handkerchief, damping it with her tongue, turning his head this way and that, dabbing away at the kiss marks, all the while laughing at him, hugging him, whispering into his ear. Pete playing up to her, hair tousled, blushing like a bridegroom on his wedding night, his free hand trailing a bottle of champagne. The man at the desk had given them a sour look and waved them through.

But there was nothing to celebrate. Pete was broke – bombed out. He was a few years short of forty and had nothing to show for it. And he was frightened – scared to find himself promoted into the big boys' league from the hundreds of petty fraudsters who clog up the unwieldy Interpol database. His activities had come to the notice of Mike Marlin. Detective Inspector Marlin – 'Spike' to his few friends and a host of enemies – had won a formidable reputation at Criminal Intelligence.

One of Pete's victims had been on the point of making a large donation to the Police Benevolent Fund. When Pete had taken him to the cleaners, the man had withdrawn his offer. It had come to Marlin's ears and the DI announced that henceforth he would take a personal interest in Peter Vance's activities, interest that would only cease when a heavy cell door clanged behind the scoundrel.

Karen had lost count of the times that she had kept him the right side of that door. He didn't know, wouldn't admit to himself how much he needed her, relied on her. That was dangerous. She used to warn him, 'The trouble with you, Pete, is that you can see six steps ahead but you need me to get you over the other five.'

'No liqueurs, Bruford, thank you. Just black coffee and we'll take it next door. Hold my calls for the next hour.' Vance stood up. 'It's back to work for us, old son. Karen is going to talk us through the tax angles. We can't have a client of ours putting his hand in his pocket to keep some finance minister in johnnies.' He laughed for all of them and settled back in a large armchair.

On the corner of the bar there was a model flagpole mounted on a silver base with a box of miniature flags beside it. 'It's Pete's little toy,' Karen explained, seeing Caswell's look of bafflement.

'Rather childish, I agree,' Vance admitted. 'Karen and I do a lot of sailing together. They are the international maritime signal flags. I stick a flag on the pole–'

'To infuriate me,' Karen broke in. 'We'll be having a disagreement and he thinks it will be amusing to see me lose my temper.'

'I know what the red one stands for. It's the same as the warning flag on a firing range. *"Keep clear – am discharging explosives"*,' said Caswell, turning them over in the box.

'You will find that one near the top,' Vance joked. 'It's had so much use it's wearing out fast.' He reached down beside his chair for a heavy volume and beckoned to Caswell to join them at the table.

Karen flicked through the reports quickly. She knew the jargon and had picked up enough knowledge over the years to pass muster. An hour later they had reached a decision. Vance leaned forward to shake the hand of his latest client. 'Then it's settled, James. Monte Carlo – here we come!' Karen passed a map of the town across the table and Vance ran an expert finger across it. 'The bank we use, James, is tucked away in a quiet side street. I know the manager from way back – Jean Baptiste – he'll look after you. You could fly out there next week and have a chat with Jean over lunch. He'll probably take you to *Le Pêcheur* – right on the front – they do a superb langouste.'

Caswell hesitated. 'You are sure that Monsieur Baptiste is ... discreet?'

'*Discreet!* Your secrets are safer with him than with the Pope. And his staff are the same. Don't give it another thought.' He leaned forward and put a hand on Caswell's arm. 'You'll have a packet of fun in Monte, old son – I really envy you. Why people go skulking off to Jersey or Guernsey, I can't imagine. Nothing to do but ride up and down the sands and most of the donkeys are the two-legged sort.'

Caswell looked around for Karen who had left the room for some minutes, but at that moment she reappeared with an envelope. 'It's not sealed, James. All the information on the bank is there and the letter you asked for.'

'Commit as much as possible to memory,' Vance advised him. 'The prisons are full of people who keep careful records.'

Caswell read the letter quickly. 'It's exactly what I wanted.' He shook hands with his hosts. 'I cannot thank you both enough. You've got me out of a dreadful jam. But more than that,' he looked shyly from one to the other, 'I feel that I have made two new friends.'

Karen gave him a brisk smile and, moving away a little, stretched out a hand to the vase to straighten one of the lilies. Vance put an arm around Caswell's shoulders. 'Karen and I feel the same, old son. I don't want to come the Good Samaritan all over you, but when you can give a mate a leg-up, it makes it all so much more worthwhile.' He looked at his watch. 'Come, Karen, New York has just opened and I believe we have two more appointments this afternoon.'

'I'm sorry. I'm keeping you. I'll be on my way.' Caswell turned towards the door.

'Forgive us, James, but time marches on. We'll see you to the lift. Give us a call in a week or two and let us know how you are getting on.'

Peter Vance and Karen waited in silence until they heard the lift reach the bottom. Then they returned to the drawing room and closed the door behind them. Vance walked over to the windows and stood by the curtain looking out over the square.

'How did I do?' he asked, turning to her. 'Pretty good, wouldn't you say?'

'I thought you were unnecessarily cruel.'

'Cruel!' He sounded genuinely surprised.

'All that crap about Jean Baptiste.'

'It was all part of the patter. I thought you were enjoying it.'

'Well, I wasn't.'

'I thought it was inspired. The name came to me just like *that*! He snapped his fingers. His eyes searched her face as he lowered his great head and she almost expected to see him paw the ground like a bull on the point of charging. 'You're not going broody over the young man – not, by any chance, allowing it to affect your judgement?'

'*Of course not, Pete!* Don't be absurd. Caswell's nothing to me.' She had spoken with more vehemence than she intended and she wondered if she was colouring. In an even tone she went on, 'It's just that all that blarney about lunch at *Le Pêcheur* seemed over the top.' She giggled. 'The poor bugger will spend the whole week dreaming about his langouste.'

'I thought you'd see the funny side of it.' Vance chewed at the inside of his cheek as if still troubled by something and then seemed to dismiss it. He removed his coat, opened his collar and threw his tie over the back of a chair.

Karen cleared the coffee cups from the table and took them over to the bar.

'Why don't you leave that for Bruford?' Vance asked irritably. 'It's his job. You're so damn fidgety this afternoon. *What's got into you?*'

Karen turned her head. 'That money in your account, Pete. There must be over two million quid. Is it all in one heap?'

'Sure it is. Everything we've got and everything we've made on this trip. Why? What's eating you?'

Karen crossed her arms tight about her, clasping her elbows. 'I don't know, Pete. Everything's worrying me. All this hanging around. It's beginning to get me down.' She ran over to him. 'Pete, let's forget Caswell. We've made a pile of money here but we're running out of time. The thought of another three days…'

A little shiver ran through her. 'It's giving me bad vibes. Come on, Pete! What do you say we take a flight out tonight?'

'*Tonight!* And write off Caswell's money! *Not likely!* Not while I'm holding a cheque for two hundred and fifty big ones in my hot little hand! *Have you gone crazy!*'

Karen stepped back from him, her eyes searching his face, looking for something and finding it gone. 'Are you sure you aren't losing your touch – getting old and careless?'

'*Like hell I am!*' Vance spoke sharply but he looked discomforted.

'You used to have an instinct which I trusted. You could feel the ground moving under your feet when to me it felt as solid as rock. I don't mind admitting I've got the jitters. Why is it so quiet? The phone hardly ever rings. *Why not*? We've been sitting on the punters' money for two to three weeks. They may be green but they're not idiots. Some of those guys must be getting jumpy. Why don't they call us to check it's all kosher?'

He laughed. 'They do. They check all the time. They are as nervous as a cat in a fur shop.'

She stared at him. 'What d'you mean?'

'I've rerouted their calls. It's wonderful what you can do with the telephone these days. They think they are calling their bank manager in Grand Cayman or Bermuda – or wherever – but they go straight through to Sam in Nassau.'

'*That old soak*!'

'Be fair, Karen. Sam is a reformed character since we got him off the rum. He's been well briefed.'

'OK. Sam can stall them for a few days but they are bound to fly out to count their money.'

'Of course they will. But they won't go until next week. I made sure of that by making them a present of their air tickets – and booking the flights. First class with all the trimmings. I hope they have plenty to eat and drink on the journey because they may be living a bit rough when they get to the other end.'

Karen threw back her head and laughed. 'The poor suckers will have to doss down at the airport.'

Vance was writing out a fax for the bank manager. 'That cheque I gave Caswell – there's no point in taking chances. I'm going to tell Quinton to put a stop on it. Smart as a whip, that chap. When I say jump – *he jumps*! And so he should. God knows he's done well enough out of me.'

Karen waved a hand in the direction of the office. 'What are you going to do?'

'With all that ironmongery next door? I'll send it back to the suppliers. A van will be here at six tomorrow morning before people are up and about.'

'They will be overjoyed to have that lot thrown back at them.'

'They left it here on approval. It wasn't approved. That's business. It's a tough world.'

'And Bruford?'

'He can give us a hand packing up the rest of the place. Then he'll be paid off.'

'Can you trust him to keep quiet?'

'Can we trust him,' Vance corrected her. 'Yes, I think we can. He's done very nicely out of us on this trip.' He took out his pocketbook and squinted at Caswell's cheque tucked between the folds.

'Shouldn't you pay that in?'

'Yes. I'll send the fax and then go straight to the bank.'

'How long will it take to clear?'

'If Quinton keeps his foot on the loud pedal – and I'll see he does – it will be cleared by mid-morning on Friday. At noon, I'll empty the account and wire the money offshore by electronic transfer. We'll cut off the phones, get the cars back to the hire company, return the keys to the agent – and then we'll blow.'

'Where are we going?'

'All in good time, Karen. Come, there's a lot to do.'

3

It was Thursday evening. Suitcases were lined up in the hall and in the drawing room the furniture, save for two armchairs, had been covered in dust sheets. The smaller ornaments had been packed away and the shelves in the bar were empty. A solitary bottle of rye whisky flanked by a pair of tumblers stood on the counter.

'The place looks like a transit camp,' Karen said sourly. 'The story of my life – it's all around me.' She chewed at a fingernail like a fractious child.

Vance parked his notebook on the arm of the chair, crossed to the bar and waved the bottle. Taking her little shrug for acceptance, he poured out two large measures. Karen took the glass from him and knocked back the spirit in a series of gulps.

'*Whoa!* Steady on, Karen!' Vance protested. 'I don't want to carry you out of here tomorrow.' He walked over to her and bent down to kiss her but at the last moment she averted her face a fraction and he missed her lips. '*What's got into you all of a sudden?*' He returned to where he had left the bottle, grabbed it by the neck and refilled his glass. 'I thought you wanted to go to bed?'

'Well, I don't.'

'Why not? It's only seven o'clock. We've done a lot today. It's workers' playtime. A good screw would improve your temper and give me an appetite for supper.'

Karen tossed her head angrily, swinging her hair across her eyes. 'How could any woman resist a line like that?'

'We've known each other too long for chat-up lines.'

'Too long for everything, I sometimes feel.'

Vance lowered the glass from his mouth and stared at her. 'What's that supposed to mean?'

'Oh, I don't know, Pete,' she replied wearily, 'let's not quarrel – not tonight.'

Vance stepped forward and seized her by the shoulder, his fingers slackening only a little as she opened her mouth to cry out. 'Not tonight or any night, partner,' he said softly. 'All I want to know is what you meant by what you said.' *Women and their bloody emotions*. This job wasn't finished yet. Why couldn't she wait until they had cleared out before she came apart at the seams?

Karen twisted away from him, putting her hand on a chair as if to help herself regain balance, swivelling it a few inches so that the bulk of it came between them. Now she rested her hands on the back and leaned forward a little. 'How long have we been together, Pete?'

Vance rolled his eyes upwards and made a play of counting off on his fingers, 'I don't know, Karen – six years, six and a half maybe.'

'It's over seven, Pete.'

Vance blew the air out of his cheeks. 'So it's over seven. Big deal.'

'It is for me. Seven years that I've sunk into our ... partnership. For me that's quite an investment.'

Vance frowned. 'I don't know about investment. You didn't bring a penny to the party – you were almost as broke as I was when we met.'

'We aren't talking about money–'

'Not talking about money?' Vance snorted. 'So what have we been doing together if it's not–'

'You know exactly what I mean.'

'Alright,' his voice rose, 'so life isn't just about money, but the stuff is bloody important if you haven't got any. And you, Karen my sweet, would be the first to complain if I bought your clothes from the charity shop.'

'You don't dress me. I pay my way.'

'So you do,' Vance conceded, 'we both do. We make a good team – the best there is – so I can't understand what the hell you're whingeing about.'

'You know very well, Pete,' Karen said quietly, 'and try to keep your voice down. There are other people living in this house and we are not in a business where it pays to advertise.'

Vance puckered his lower lip like a child who has been scolded. *'I'm sorry, Karen, but sometimes you really drive me mad!'*

'You shouldn't make promises that you have no intention of keeping.'

'What promises, Karen?' Vance blustered, in an effort to dam the laughter threatening to burst its banks. 'Surely you didn't take that seriously, did you?'

'Yes. I did. I believed you. I thought that lies were things you kept for your clients.'

'Karen, that's not–'

'I didn't think that it was just a ploy to get me into your bed.'

'It wasn't just a ploy, Karen. I missed you. I wanted you. What do you think I'm made of – ice cubes?' Vance walked over to the bar, selected a flag from the box, a horizontal yellow strip top and bottom, a wider red band between them. He fixed it to the top of the pole.

Karen stuck out her tongue. 'I know – *"Keep clear of me!"* That's how I felt. You were lucky it wasn't worse.'

'This bad?' With a teasing lift of his eyebrows, Vance pulled out another. Two red, two white squares. *You are standing into danger!*

'Not far off.' Then, catching the grin on his face, 'But it isn't funny, Pete – you can't be serious about anything.'

'I am being serious, Karen. What's more serious than being put in the deep-freeze for weeks on end – and just think what separate bedrooms have been costing us in some of these hotels. There, Karen, now you're smiling. Don't pretend you're not. You can't keep a straight face.'

'If I didn't laugh at myself, I would cry. I'm such a perfect little fool.' She took a deep breath and held it, forcing back the tears. 'It wasn't fair, Pete.'

'No more unfair than locking your door every night. After all we've–'

'You had broken our contract. That was the penalty. As a businessman, I would have thought you could understand that. Anyway, you had all the girls you needed. Trawling through the clubs every night – you loved it. Remember those girls in Miami? Those silky brown bodies poured into Lycra pants, roller-blading up and down the boulevards, looking for a new stud?' She sighed. 'I envy men sometimes. I bet those girls were great in bed. No, you didn't need me, Pete. You had a marvellous time.'

Vance looked uncomfortable. 'It wasn't the same, Karen.'

'Of course it wasn't the same. You had to pay for it.'

'You know that wasn't what I meant. You're the only woman I've ever fancied.'

Karen laughed. 'That is the most sublime crap.'

'I didn't mean...'

'I'm sure you didn't.'

'Karen, *listen* a moment!'

Karen arched her eyebrows. 'Well, I am listening.'

'I'm not going to tell you until you stop looking so po-faced.'

'Anyone who's had to listen to your fairy tales all these years becomes just a little cynical.'

'All I ask is a fair hearing,' said Vance sullenly. 'That's the least you can do.'

'Go on then. Nobody's stopping you.'

'You know that I've worked like a dog these seven years, Karen, and I've done it for–'

'Not for me, you haven't!' Karen flung back her head. 'Oh, Pete, that's too rich. You weren't going to say that you had done it all for me. You bring tears to my eyes. Why, you've never even trusted me with a joint account.'

Vance walked over to the window, his hands clenched tight, his arms tight against his sides. 'Don't push too hard, Karen,' he said, turning back to her. 'I'm not nice when I'm pushed too hard.'

'That's why these conversations are so futile,' Karen retorted. Fear gave her a sort of desperate courage. 'Just when we begin getting somewhere, I start looking out my tin helmet.'

'I'm sorry. You know I don't mean to hurt you. Sometimes I lose control. I just can't help myself.'

'Aren't you afraid that one day I might up sticks and walk out on you?'

Vance regarded her gravely. 'Yes, I am sometimes afraid of that. I was trying to tell you, Karen, that if I've made something of myself these past years, it's because of you. Life had flushed me down the pan and you pulled me out. I wanted to show–'

'You wanted someone to admire you, cheer you on, pat you on the back, pick you up when you fell down, put some sticking plaster on your knee, whisper in your ear, *"Go on Pete! You're the best. You can do it!"*'

'You may mock, Karen, but we've got to hang in there. Another year, even six months ... we're approaching lift-off! *Don't spoil things now!*'

'You promised me that Miami would wind things up. Then we'd call it a day. You ratted on the deal. Then it was London. That was the big one. The very last hit. Now you tell me to wait while you stitch up another bunch of idiots.'

Exasperated, Vance flung his hands in the air. 'Have you got a better plan, Karen? What do you want me to do? Scuttle off to the Registry Office and sign up? Buy you a cosy little flat off the Finchley Road? Settle down and have two-point-four kids like the rest of the mugs?'

'And what's so terrible about that?' Karen flared back at him.

'*You can't mean it!* What's happened to the Karen I used to know? What's happened to the old buccaneering spirit? We've got to think big. We're not just a couple of hustlers out to rip off a few saps!'

'Isn't that just what we have been doing?'

'Of course it is, but money is just the beginning. Can't you see that, Karen? If one has enough money, one can have as many lives as a rich man has suits in his wardrobe – and change them as often. There's so much of the world I haven't seen, so many things I haven't done.' In his excitement Vance was pacing up and down the room. 'I would like to live in a monastery high up in the Himalayas, talk with priests and sages–'

'You would have to polish up your soul a little before you went.'

'Or buy an ocean-going yacht and have a crack at the Admiral's Cup, maybe sail to South America, trek into the interior.'

'You had better be quick while there still is an interior.'

'I would like to search out remote corners of the earth, learn the secrets of primitive tribes–'

'They'd make you team captain, Pete.'

Vance shook his head impatiently. '*It's almost within reach, Karen!* Can't you understand that? After all these years, *it's so close*. I would like to have my own laboratory, the latest equipment, the best brains that money could buy and beat the rest of the world to solving one of the last, perhaps the greatest mystery in science.'

'So?'

'*So everything!* Unlock the cipher of our genetic make-up! Pick the winning line in the lottery of life! Discover what permutation produces genius, what makes a Beethoven, a Napoleon, an Einstein – and leaves the rest of us pygmies with a dud ticket.'

'It's too late to wish your life all over again.'

Vance swivelled on his heel, his great chest heaving. *'It's never too late, Karen!'* He drove a great fist into the palm of his hand with tremendous force. *'Not till they nail the lid down on top of you!* If you want it enough, you can have all the lives you can handle.' He glared at her, his mouth working furiously. 'But this means nothing to you, Karen. You want us to lead the same arid, downtrodden little life as the rest. Just a brighter shade of grey because we can afford to buy our groceries at Harrods instead of Tesco.'

'I thought you just wanted to be rich. That at least was straightforward. I could cope with that. What do I find now? That money isn't enough, that you are running after some new fantasy.'

'What's life about, Karen, if it isn't about moving the end of the rainbow? For most people, the rainbow's end means paying off the mortgage after thirty years, having the grandchildren around to Sunday lunch. If that's all you want out of life, Karen, you've been knocking on the wrong door.'

'Now you tell me!'

He stretched out his arms to her, his voice softening. 'Don't be like that, Karen.'

Karen rubbed her eyes with the tips of her fingers. 'I don't know, Pete. All I know is that I'm tired of it. Tired of all the dreams. Tired of living out of a suitcase, tired of running, tired of wondering where I'm going to be next week or who I'm going to be the week after. We've got enough dummy passports between us for a game of poker.'

'Can you really see yourself, Karen, pushing a buggy round the supermarket, hanging the washing on the line? You would go out of your mind within six months.'

'I think you are talking about yourself – not about me.'

'But you're so young still – you're not yet thirty.'

'Twenty-eight next month. *Twenty-eight going on fifty!* A woman's body isn't like a man's, Pete – as I'm sure you've noticed. And it's not just a trampoline. It's got a job to do. And that doesn't get easier as you get older.'

Vance sighed. 'We seem to be going round in circles. What's wrong with what we've got, Karen? It's a better life than you had.'

'When you fell over me? That wouldn't be difficult.'

'You're tired, Karen. What you want is a holiday. We'll make time for it. You'll see, you'll feel quite different. Sunshine, blue seas, a good-looking fellow like me to keep a smile on your face.'

'I want a home, Pete, and I want children. I've never had a home. Not a real home.'

'Your mother's house – wasn't that a home?'

'My mother ran a boarding house in Hove.'

'Hove was it? She's come down in the world. When we first met you told me she lived in Brighton – in the hotel business.'

'You're hardly one to talk – all that bull you gave James ... James Caswell ... about your so-called career.'

'It worked, didn't it? It always does.'

'Does it, Pete? I don't know. Sometimes I can't remember what's true and what's a lie. It's all muddled up in my head. Sometimes I find myself thinking what a glamorous life my father has – a captain on a cruise liner – I've told that story so often I can't think of him–'

'*As a barman on a cross-channel ferry!*' Vance blew out his cheeks contemptuously.

But Karen wasn't listening. She rested her elbows on the back of the chair, her chin cupped in her hands. 'I can just see him in his white tropical uniform, swanning around the West Indies in a great big liner – palm trees, blue lagoons, silver sand, the outline of some exotic island, tomorrow's landfall showing black against the setting sun.' Her eyes closed and she smiled dreamily. 'And a night full of stars. Beautiful women in long silk dresses drifting in from the rail, a faint aroma of perfume, something light, subtle, enticing. The sparkle of wonderful diamonds ... somewhere a dance band playing...'

'You've forgotten the men – half a dozen paunchy car salesmen in shirt sleeves.'

'*Oh, no!* I don't see them like that at all.'

'How do you see them?'

'The men ...' she reflected for a moment, 'men who are still in the hunt, whatever it is they are after – adventure, opportunity – one last fling before the fire goes out of them. Men who don't play the percentage game. Men who see something they want and go for it – put everything on a single number. That's what makes them exciting – and dangerous.' She turned back to him. *'And bloody impossible to live with!'*

Vance laughed. 'Nonsense, Karen. You love it. You're a gypsy at heart. Do you remember that old rust bucket we picked up in Honfleur and sailed down to Gibraltar? Those night crossings to Tangier – no moon, blowing half a gale and a dirty-big sea that kept the customs boys tucked up in bed – cheap NAAFI cigarettes and Spanish brandy that tasted like paint stripper? *Christ! We've had some good times!'*

Karen shook her head. 'It's no good, Pete. I've changed. I've been part of somebody's caravan train since I was sixteen ... since I left home ... or what passed for home.'

'Serves you right for sleeping with the lodger,' Vance said flippantly.

'I never–'

'Don't tell me you've forgotten Luke?' Vance's mouth dropped in mock astonishment. 'Leg-over Luke? The old derelict who lived with your mother? Rent-free I shouldn't wonder and paid the old bat in kind. It's your best story. It always used to crease me. You remember, Karen? He got small parts in the local rep when he was sober enough to stand upright. Always legless by Saturday night and spent Sunday pissing it away over the end of the pier. Now he was a character.'

'He was a bastard!' Karen spat the words at him.

'Probably that as well but his story was that he was a sleepwalker. You should have locked your door at night.'

'I did lock it. My mother gave him a key. She just wanted an excuse to kick me out.'

'Then Gary took you under his wing – in a manner of speaking. You remember Gary? The road manager with that pop group?'

'Gary didn't give me a home.' She closed her eyes. They were always on the move. A different gig every night. The heat, the noise, the blinding lights, the glistening bodies with their mesmeric swaying, the white, stupefied faces, the smell of stale beer, sweat and vomit, and then back to the caravan and Gary thumping into her like a kitchen boy with a slab of veal. She could never pass a restaurant kitchen and hear the slap of the mallet on the raw meat without thinking of Gary.

Vance looked at her. She was miles away, not here with him where she ought to be. Sometimes he thought she did it on purpose, as if she knew it riled him. 'I bet Gary put a few dents in your front bumper,' he sneered. He regretted it as soon as he had said it but Karen had this knack of bringing out the worst in him.

Karen crossed the room and went into the hall.

'Where do you think you're going?' he shouted after her.

She reappeared in the doorway. 'If you'll tell me which passports we are using and where we are going, Pete,' she said quietly, 'I will get the luggage labels written out.'

'No, no. Leave all that to me. They go on when we check in the baggage – and not a second before. *Don't you remember anything you've been taught?*'

'I'm sorry, Pete.' She turned away.

'And make sure there's nothing in those suitcases that will put a tag on us – go through all the clothes–'

'I've already done it,' she protested.

'*Well, do it again!* Turn out the pockets. Make sure there's no credit card receipts, theatre tickets or restaurant bills. You should know the score by this time.' The last twenty-four hours were always the worst on a job like this. Why did she have to play him up just now? She needed knocking into line.

4

It was Friday morning and a quarter of an hour before midday. Vance took a last look around the office. Save for a single telephone on the window sill, it was bare. Stripped out. The walls were scuffed where the equipment had been removed and the letting agents would probably be puzzled by the multitude of electric points. No doubt they would write to their client in Hong Kong to tell him that they had put in hand a complete redecoration of the apartment and to expect a fat bill in due course. Too bad, but the man had got six months rent in advance so he shouldn't squeal too loudly.

At that moment the telephone rang. It was Roy Kerr. 'Is Karen there?' he whispered.

'No.' Vance told him. 'She's not. She was out early this morning. She had a lot to do. We've got to be away from here in a couple of hours.'

'I've got to see you, Pete! *It's urgent!*'

'*Now?* You must be joking! There's nothing to talk about! Our mutual client has done the necessary. You'll get your commission. You were lucky to get through to me. All the phones will be off the moment I hang up.'

'Then you're the one who was lucky,' Roy hissed.

'What do you mean?' Instinctively Vance looked down into the street but all seemed quiet and peaceful. The sky was a dull grey. It looked like rain.

'I can't tell you. Not like this. Suppose we had a woodpecker on the line?'

'Can't you come to me?'

'No! I'm not coming there!' Roy's voice rose in panic.

Vance looked at his watch. '*I'll be with you in twenty minutes but it bloody well better be important.* I've a fax that's got to go to my bank. I'll send it from your office.' He slammed the receiver back on the hook. Roy was becoming a liability. His nerves were all over the place. He couldn't be trusted any longer. Next time he came to London, he would look for a replacement.

He grabbed an umbrella from the stand in the hall, took the lift to the ground floor and then stood in the doorway looking up and down the street. A few drops of rain were starting to fall. His luck was in. A taxi was dropping a fare at the next block some fifty yards away. He leaned out under cover of the umbrella and waved. There was a flash of headlights in acknowledgement.

'All right for some, ain't it, guv?' the cabbie grumbled as he yanked the passenger door open. He jerked his head backwards as they moved off and Vance turned and squinted through the rear window. There was a blue Vauxhall saloon parked against the railings under the plane trees.

'Unmarked police car,' the driver said laconically. 'Four of the lads from Gerald Row just sitting there having a smoke. Why don't they get off their backsides and catch a few villains? What with all this street crime you'd think they'd be spoilt for choice.'

Vance gave the man directions and edged along the back seat until he was squeezed into the corner. The cabbie glanced at his passenger in the mirror. Obviously a businessman. He preferred them. They had better things to do than give you a lot of chat and they tipped better. His radio squawked. 'Soho Square,' he reported, 'fifteen minutes if we get a decent run.'

As they moved away from the road junction another police car travelling very fast, lights flashing but no siren, took the traffic lights at red and turned down the slip road they had just left. *Shit*! Instinctively Vance slipped a hand to his inside pocket. Passport and tickets were there. But forget going back for the luggage. That was a write-off.

A little over twelve minutes later Vance paid off the cab. He waited until it was round the square and out of sight before cutting through a quiet side street. He found a telephone kiosk. He must warn Karen not to go back to Eaton Square. They were both carrying one of the new Motorola pagers.

He called the GPO. Bleep her three times at ten-second intervals, he told them. The prearranged signal was for emergencies. It meant, *'Do not return to base! Urgent! Advise present location!'* The operator kept interrupting him. 'We only have limited coverage, caller.' He put the receiver down. He could feel the sweat running down his arms and his shirt sticking to his back.

He played with the telephone directory while he looked down the street. Roy's office was about thirty yards away on the same side. Across the road there was a surface car park fenced with crude boarding and a desultory attendant propped against his rickety shack.

The pedestrians seemed to be going about their business, no lurking in shop doorways or studying their reflections in the plate-glass windows. Two teenagers in jeans and trainers pushing their way through a curtain encouraged by a sign warning them that they might be offended by the goods displayed inside. A small Italian restaurant, a grocers and, upstairs, a dance studio. A window advertising Swedish massage.

A curtain twitched but in this area they often did. Down to the street again. Cars parked nose to tail like so many dirty dogs. Nobody sitting in the back seat cutting peepholes in his newspaper. He emerged, unrolled the umbrella once more and kept it low over his head. The rain was falling steadily now. He took it as a good omen. But if things got tricky, Roy had a door at the rear which led into the back of a radio shop. He arrived to find the front door opening to him.

'Hello Roy? Where are you hiding? Ah, behind the door. Things as bad as that, are they? And where's Miss Muffet?'

'Out.' Roy led the way to the meeting room. He was puffing with the exertion of descending a short flight of stairs or perhaps it was nerves. 'I sent her out for some sandwiches.'

'Not for me, I trust. I never–'

'Tuna and pineapple – how can you resist?'

'Easily.'

'Have a chair. You're going to need–'

'I'll stand. I'm in a hurry.'

'Well, don't fall down in a dead faint and then say I didn't warn–'

'Let's have it, Roy – whatever it is.'

Roy pushed two stubby fingers into the breast pocket of his jacket and extracted something. He slid it across the table.

Vance leaned over the table, framing the small photographic print with his large hands. He raised his head and stared at Roy. A livid streak ran along the line of his cheekbone as if he had been struck across the face with a whip. 'When did you get this?'

'This morning ... in the post ... it's only just arrived.'

'Who sent it?' he whispered.

Roy swallowed hard. 'The barman at this place in Marbella ... you know...' To his consternation, he found himself stammering.

Vance's jaw had dropped like the trap falling beneath the feet of a condemned man. 'No. I don't know,' he said slowly. 'You tell me...'

'You and Karen were there in April–'

'Only for the night – we stopped over on our way to Tenerife.'

Roy raked his fingers through his scalp, disturbing small flakes of dandruff which drifted down and settled on his shoulders. 'Just for one night? Are you quite sure, Pete?'

Vance went very still. 'Karen wasn't very well – or so she told me. No, I misled you. She stayed on for two days and then joined me in Las Palmas.'

'Ah, well...'

'Ah, well!' Vance snarled back at him, his top lip curling away from the gums like a savage dog. 'Ah, well...'

'I'm sorry, Pete ... I only meant–'

'I know what you meant. It's as plain as the balls on a dog. She met Caswell in Marbella. They may even have planned to meet there.' Vance clamped his eyes shut like a man stepping naked under an ice-cold shower. 'And I, like a dimwit, left them to it.'

'It wasn't your–'

'It was my fault. But what the fuck were they doing there – *besides bonking each other stupid?*' He opened his eyes very wide. 'Were the two of them trying to set me up?'

'A funny way of going about it–'

'Why funny? What was so funny–'

'What I mean is ... if I was going to rip–' He broke off.

'Go on!' Vance roared at him. 'Don't mind me!'

'If I was going to rip someone off, I wouldn't start by giving him a cheque for a quarter of a million quid.' Almost light-headed with relief at having reached the end of the sentence with his limbs still intact, he went on. 'That cheque he gave you – you said it cleared okay?'

'No problem. My bank rang me to confirm an hour ago.'

'That puts Karen in the clear. If she and Caswell were in cahoots, she would have warned him. She would never have let him meet you.'

'So why did she pretend that she had never met Caswell?'

'Because she had ... because they had–'

'Because they had screwed each other's arse off. For Lord's sake, Roy, don't jerk me around.'

'Well, I suppose that was it,' Roy muttered. 'Karen had a guilty conscience.'

Vance's eyes rested on him. 'And after what they ... did together ... she still walked Caswell into that trap?' His teeth were clenched tight, chewing the words out of shape. 'You *really* believe that?'

Roy shuffled his feet uncomfortably. 'Yes. I do. Nothing else makes sense.'

Vance tugged at the lobe of an ear. 'Perhaps you are right. Perhaps it was just a two-night affair.'

'Did you give Caswell your own cheque? You usually do.'

'Of course. *It's the clincher.* How many people do you know have held a cheque for that amount in their hand. He took the hook and the line with it. They all do. I put a stop on it within a few minutes of him leaving. I tell you, Roy, I didn't give him an opening – not there, I didn't.'

'And Karen knew about the stop?'

'Yes.'

'And he hasn't presented your cheque?'

'No.'

'Well, Pete, that wraps it up. Obviously Karen never told him. If she had, he would have stopped his own cheque and lobbed yours through your window with a brick tied to it.'

Vance almost smiled. 'Then the show's back on the road. Caswell believes everything's fine and dandy and his money is winging its way to Monaco.'

'When does he get his big surprise?'

'At five o'clock. That's four hours and forty minutes from now. He's expecting the bank in Monte to call but of course they won't. Then he'll get the shits – and things will be a bit lively for a day or two.'

'And what about me, Pete? Have you thought of that? Caswell may–'

'Caswell won't trouble you. He'll have a bit of a moan. So should I in his shoes. If he gets stroppy, remind him that he was breaking the law. The courts take a very dim view of people who try to escape their obligations.' Vance picked up the photograph and stared at it once more. Roy could hear his jaws working as if he was about to put the object between his teeth and shred it.

'How did the photograph come to be taken?'

'The hotel was producing a new brochure. Perhaps they needed a few new faces.'

'Karen doesn't like having her photograph taken. The last time that happened, the camera fetched up at the bottom of the pool.'

'She probably didn't know. It looks as if it was taken from a room in the hotel.'

Vance held up the print to the light. 'You may be right. I can just see the top of a Martini umbrella in the foreground.' With a scowl he pushed it into his pocket. 'How did the barman get hold of it?'

'I guess that Pedro found them and was flicking through–'

'*I bet he was!* A friend of yours, was he Roy?' That bikini of Karen's wouldn't cover a stick of barley sugar.

'*No, Pete!* He's just a contact. I swear it. He gave Caswell my card. When he found this photo of the guy, he sent it to me. He just wanted to remind me that I owed him one.'

'It's a pity he didn't send the photograph a few days ago, it might have saved you and me a lot of trouble.' And Karen a mountain of grief.

'What about Karen? You won't...'

'Leave Karen to me.'

'She's made a bloody fool out of me – I feel–'

'*Who gives a rap what you feel?*' Vance snapped back at him. 'And must you keep sneaking off to that window? You give me the screaming ab-dabs.'

'Sorry, Pete, but Linda's back late and there's no one watching the screen.'

Vance closed the distance between them in a pair of swift strides. He grabbed Roy by the shoulder and whirled him around to face him. '*What is it with this bloody screen, Roy?* What have you got in this building?'

Roy wriggled helplessly, his face as grey as old porridge. 'Just a few pills,' he muttered. *'Pete! Let me go!'*

'What sort of pills?' Vance hoisted him by his shoulders so that he was standing on tiptoe.

'Just a few happy pills, Pete,' said Roy, his front teething edging forward like actors uncertain of their reception at the end of a performance. '*Nothing heavy!* You know I wouldn't mess with that.'

'Is that the whole story?'

'Not ... not quite.'

'Well then?'

'Some of the stuff isn't mine. I have been looking after it for one of the big boys.'

Vance released him with a vicious shove against the end of the table. 'I knew you were stupid, Roy, but I credited you with enough sense to keep out of that game. If the cops–' He glanced at his watch. '*Oh, to hell with it*! I haven't got time to waste on you. I've got to get a fax to Quinton at the bank. It's already late.'

Roy led the way to the stairs. 'I'll send it right away, Pete.'

'No, you won't. I'll send it. It's confidential. You watch your precious screen.' He would go straight to the airport and try for an earlier flight. The coppers would break into the penthouse and sit on his luggage like Paddington Bear waiting for him to come back.

Karen would have to take her chance. He was almost sorry that he had warned her. If she didn't get the message and went to Eaton Square, she would probably spend the night in Holloway. Otherwise she had her passport but no ticket and little money. She couldn't follow him. She hadn't a clue where he was going. She was all washed up. If she wanted a shoulder to cry on, she could run off to Caswell. She would be lucky if he could find the price of a packet of Kleenex. They deserved each other.

Roy was bent over a large portable radio. He extended the aerial and started playing with the knobs. Vance took a sheet of paper from an inside pocket and fed it into the fax machine. He watched it slide through and as he picked up the acknowledgement slip and tucked it away in the folds of his wallet, he let out a long sigh of relief. The last piece in the jigsaw had been slotted into place. Quinton didn't hang about. Within a minute or so two million pounds would be in Mexico. He would leave a few thousand in the London account. It might come in useful. There was always another day.

Travelling west, he would be in Mexico City before the bars closed. He had booked the best room at The Four Seasons. He'd find himself a classy lady, someone who could walk into a room on his arm and stop the conversation as dead as if the chandelier had fallen down. Trained up, she could supply more than a little strenuous relaxation; she would be a business asset.

In Mexico there was a man he wanted to meet – one of the few men in the world to whom he would defer. Wealthy beyond imagination, this man deployed his money as Napoleon his armies. No calculation of where power resided could discount his influence. Governments – profligate, self-serving or corrupt – lived in dread of him. He was a man in a million. Vance would bring his plans to this man, sit at his table. One day ... one day soon ... they would talk as equals. Peter Vance was ready for the next stage of his life.

As for Karen, in a month she would have given Caswell the heave-ho, chucked him out with the unpaid laundry bill. Then she would try to crawl back. He might take her – on his terms – or he might not. It depended how the other girl shaped up. He would run the two against each other – twice the chances and double the fun, like playing two hands at blackjack.

Vance took a long, hard look at the screen. Nothing stirring. Roy pressed a button on the radio. 'Fantastic what you can pick up on this gadget – all the police frequencies, even the control tower at Heathrow!'

'I haven't got time, Roy, I'm on my way.'

'News bulletins all round the clock.' He had pressed another button.

'So long, Roy, keep out of mischief.' Vance was making for the door when he stopped. He had heard the name *Jean Baptiste*. It was the name that he had given Caswell, the calling card of the phantom banker in Monte Carlo. That was careless ... he must be getting old ... where had he heard that name?

'It's only about that rotting boat. Why does that–'

'*Belt up, Roy!* I want to hear this.' Treading softly, he came back into the room. Now he knew how the name had come to him. An article in the papers some days earlier had caught his eye. The *Jean Baptiste* was a three-masted schooner anchored in the port of Marseille. It was owned by an eccentric millionaire who had recruited a small professional crew for a two-year expedition to the Pacific.

The ship's company included some thirty adventurous young people drawn from different countries and selected after intense competition. Many of them were research scientists of whom great things were expected. The ship had been ready to sail when the sponsor, a man in his late forties, had suffered a heart attack and died, leaving large unpaid bills for fitting out and provisioning the vessel. His executors had been unable to discharge these until the estate was wound up and the whole project was placed in jeopardy. In time-honoured fashion, bailiffs acting for the creditors had nailed their writs to the ship's mast – and that seemed to be that.

'Just when the expedition was on the point of being abandoned,' the newsreader was saying, 'an anonymous benefactor has made substantial funds available. All the outstanding accounts have been settled. The *Jean Baptiste* is being made ready for sea and sails on the evening tide.'

'Switch that bloody thing off!' Vance shouted at Roy. *'Ignorant bugger!* There is no tide in the Med!' To hear any more was beyond endurance. Admiration and envy battled within him. Who was this Titan who had humbled the Fates, picked up the smoking thunderbolt and hurled it down their throats? To stay behind with the rest of the human dross while a great enterprise put out on such a voyage, to linger on the shore's edge straining after it until the last splash of gold on the mast-tips tarnished and the sails clouded

into dusk, to watch night fall and the dark sea wring the last glimmer from the sky, to know that the sun would come up upon another man's dream ... it was a sword thrust to his very heart.

The telephone buzzed. Roy lunged for it. '*Linda! Where in fuck's name are you?* Not coming back? What d'you mean – *not coming back!* He hopped about the floor in an extremity of agitation. 'Frightened? *You little freak!* There's nothing to be scared about!' He held the mouthpiece away from him, staring at it as if he had hold of a cobra. 'I don't believe it,' he muttered. 'She put the phone down on me!'

Vance took the receiver from him and replaced it. 'Linda seems to have forgotten all about your sandwiches. It sounds as if she's got a new man in her life.'

'Bowker – I'll bet it's him.' Roy fished in his pocket for a grubby handkerchief and mopped his face.

'What's Bowker's vocation in life? Helping old ladies across the road? Taking kiddies to the sweet shop?'

'He's on the door at Zoe's.'

'The club muscle?'

'If there's trouble–'

'I bet there's plenty – and more on the way.' Vance smiled vindictively. He was enjoying this. He had never seen Roy in such a state. He ought to run out for some nappies. The lad was ready to fill his pants. It was most amusing. 'I'll tell you what's happened, old son. Someone's put the squeeze on your friend Bowker.' Roy winced as Vance made claws of his hands and crushed an invisible orange into liquid pulp. 'It could be one of the local dealers who's heard that there's someone filching his customers, someone who's asking to have his balls nailed to the floor with a staple gun!'

'Oh God, Pete,' Roy moaned, 'have a heart.'

'Or it could be your friendly neighbourhood copper,' Vance continued cheerfully, 'who's under a bit of pressure. The Super's wondering how old Plod can afford holidays in the Seychelles on a detective constable's pay while drugs on the street are outselling cornflakes. He's tired of hammering down doors and finding the villains sitting around playing Scrabble. He wants a bust – *now!* So old Plod better come up with a new name – *fast!*' Vance frowned to show that he was prepared to share a small fraction of the other man's misery. 'Either way, it means you're going to have visitors – *and soon!*'

Roy leaned against the wall. 'I don't feel very well.'

'This is no time to go sick. Put on your bicycle clips and start pedalling.' His hand reached for the doorknob. 'On which note I must bid you a fond–'

The telephone startled them. Roy raised the receiver to his ear and passed it over with an appalling smirk.

'It's for you, Pete.'

'For me? *Surely not!*'

'For you.'

It was Harold Quinton. 'I've been trying to reach you on your office number for the past half hour. The line is dead.'

'The engineers are working on it,' Vance told him smoothly. 'Probably some gas fitter's dropped a blowtorch down the wrong hole.' He could usually count on Quinton for a sycophantic chuckle but there wasn't a hint of response.

'I tried to page you.'

'I have had no messages.'

'I had Mr Kerr's number so–'

'Well, Harold,' Vance interposed, 'now you've found me. I'm trying to get off to the airport.'

'I got your–'

'You got my fax. It's all very straightforward.'

'Yes. That's what worried me. I got your first fax about twenty minutes ago.'

'*My first fax! Hang on, Harold*! I only sent one fax and that was about five minutes ago.'

'You did? Just the one you say? Then who sent the earlier one, because I have it right here in front of–'

'Hold on a moment, you can't–'

'*Please*, Mr Vance, let me finish. I have two facsimile messages in front of me. The first, on which I have acted, was received at twelve noon precisely – the time you told me to expect disposal instructions for the cash held in your current account. The destination of the funds was a little surprising but for a man of your very considerable wealth the instructions were ... credible. We were under an obligation to make the transfer immediately. You will recall your standing orders to us. They are explicit. Nevertheless, the circumstances were so unusual that I made every effort to reach you while our experts scrutinised the document.'

Vance had pulled so much air into his lungs that he half expected his feet to leave the ground. He was for the moment incapable of speech.

'The message,' Quinton persisted, 'was carried on your business paper and bore today's date. The typeface was consistent throughout, there were no alterations and your signature at the foot of the page was examined by our specialist before being cleared. In the absence of new instructions, we could delay no longer. The transfer was effected. It is the only time that I can remember delaying implementing an order in defiance of firm instructions, but my colleagues and I agreed that the very unusual circumstances warranted a short delay before execution.'

Delay before execution ... before execution ... execution ... execution... The room seemed to have grown very dark. There was a great rushing in Vance's ears and he had the sensation of falling, as if he had walked over the entrance to a mineshaft and stepped into emptiness ... down ... down ... down ... to an unknowable depth, conscious with some part of his mind of faint resonance from some world beyond the void. Gradually his hearing returned, sharpening into focus, and snatches of Quinton's speech became intelligible once more.

'You must, I think, concede that my colleagues and I acted with all diligence. Your appointment of two trustees to administer the fund seemed eminently sensible.'

'I did that?' Vance sneered, his five senses restored to him. 'I appointed two blatant fraudsters as trustees? Gave them a couple of million quid and sent them on a long cruise? That must have been one of my better ideas.'

'In the overall context–'

Vance cut him short. 'I'm going to the airport, Quinton. Send a copy of the fax to the Sheraton Hotel at Heathrow. I'll pick it up in an hour.'

'Where can I reach you, Mr Vance?'

'You can't!' He put the phone down.

Roy had a hand on his arm. 'Bad news?'

Vance shook him off. 'I've had better.' He buttoned up his coat. 'It was very neat. I rather underestimated our friend Mr Caswell.' And like all the best scams, it was so simple. Caswell knew where he banked and he had the number of his account. He had a letter on his business paper with a signature at the bottom of the page. He had only to erase Vance's letter with a liquid paper solution obtainable at any stationers and substitute his own instructions. The operation required care but no great skill.

If the bank had seen the original letter, they would have spotted the trick instantly. A blind man running his fingers over the paper would not have been fooled for a moment. But the bank was at a disadvantage. The paper, the key element in the deception, was their own and beyond suspicion. Without forensic equipment, they stood no chance. To the naked eye, the forgery was undetectable.

Karen had probably flown with Caswell to Marseille, leaving instructions with a secretarial bureau to send the fax to Quinton. The champagne corks would already be popping. They would be the toast of the town.

'That commission you promised, Pete…'

Vance laughed. The sound had a vicious ring to it. 'Put it down to experience, Roy.'

The telephone again. Roy picked it up with the tips of his fingers as if it carried a high-voltage charge. *'It's Karen!'* he squawked out of the side of his mouth.

'Let me have her! I'll kill that–'

Roy backed away from him. 'She doesn't want to talk to you, Pete. She's frightened–'

'So she frigging well ought to be!' Vance made another dive for the receiver and wrenched it away. 'Where are you, Karen?' His voice sounded strangely hoarse in his ears. 'Do you realise what you've done to me? When I get my hands–'

'If you threaten me, Pete, I'll put down.' In her fear, she was almost shouting as she tried to iron out the quaver in her voice. 'I'm at Marseille harbour.'

'Marseille harbour!' Just when he thought that he had reached bottom, he was still falling. 'Karen, I'm trying to control myself but I'm losing the battle.'

'Pete, please listen to me.'

'Why should I listen to you, Karen? You're poison. You're a walking contagion. You're contaminated land. They ought to fence you off from the rest of the human race, put up warning signs–'

'Pete! *Please!'*

'How could you do it, Karen? That's what I want to know.'

'Pete, I know I've got a lot to answer for but there isn't time.'

'Time is your problem, Karen, but not mine. I've got lots of time. I've got all the time in the world and I'll give my little girl one guess how I'm going to spend it.'

'Do what you like! I can't stop you if that's how you feel!'

'It is how I feel. And when I catch up with you, I am going to show you exactly how I feel. And, Karen, believe me, *I feel terrible.*'

'I took you for a bigger man. It seems I was–'

'*A bigger man!*' Vance shrilled 'You were my partner! *Remember!* We shared the good times and we shared the shit. *Remember!* We shared a bed – if you haven't already forgotten. Comrades-in-arms, that's what we were. Every other beat of my heart belonged to you – and what did you do? You cheated me, betrayed me, ruined me. How big does one have to be, for Christ's sake?'

'I don't blame you for being sore.'

'*Sore!* Oh, no! You're quite mistaken. I'm not sore. You're still thinking in inches and feet, Karen. Hot and cold. So many degrees one way or the other. Take it from me, sweetheart, I'm way beyond that. *I'm right off the end of the scale!*'

'Then I can't talk to you.'

'Talk away. Kid yourself along. You may find it helps.'

'I promise I'll tell you the truth.'

'Promise what you like. It won't change anything.'

'I admit that I deceived you over James.'

'"James", is it?' Vance sneered. 'How long has it been "James"?'

'For some time. Does it matter? He fell for me. That's the long and short of it. I was attracted to him. You were giving me a hard time…' Her voice tailed off.

'Go on.'

'I didn't lie about James. He was in trouble with the bank. He had guaranteed the loan to Rochfort Raikes.

The firm went bust. He was expecting a writ. It was all perfectly true.'

'That's a great comfort. Where is all this leading, Karen? You can save your breath if you think–'

'He and I ... were together in Marbella.'

'As if I needed reminding.'

'So you know?'

'You and Caswell were photographed at the hotel.'

'James got into conversation with some barman who gave him Roy's card. It was such bad luck.'

'The bad luck doesn't end there. The barman sent Roy the photo. It arrived this morning. Roy called me the moment he saw it.'

'I tried to persuade James not to contact you.'

'What did you tell him?'

'In the end I had to tell him the truth.'

'The whole truth? That you and I and Roy were in this together.'

'I had to. I warned him he'd be taken to the cleaners. He laughed like a drain. He said he could look after himself.'

'He spoke truly.'

'Pete, believe me – I had no hand in his plans. I never–'

'You vouched for him, Karen. You gave the enemy the password. *Shooting is too good for you!*'

'Pete! *Listen to me!* I never dreamed he could get away with it. I couldn't see how it could be done. When I asked him how much money he was after he made a joke of it – enough for a wedding present, that's what he said. There's no point in saying I'm sorry. You wouldn't believe me.'

'Oh, I believe you, Karen. In your shoes, I should feel sorry too. You can't imagine how sorry I should feel.'

'I can understand you being bitter, Pete. I can understand you wanting revenge, but you played a foul trick on me. I wanted some of my own back.'

'Some! *You've hit the jackpot!* Enjoy it while you still can!'

'You yell at me, Pete, but I wonder you can't see how alike you and James are.'

'*Alike!* That little squirt ... like me?' For a moment Vance was too astonished to go on.

'I've always thought you were clever – even brilliant on your day. James is very bright. He got the top first in Marine Biology at university. He's very ambitious. Like you, he wants an extraordinary life.'

'But not a very long one apparently.'

'Pete, I'm sure he never intended to take all the money, not at first, anyway – but when that man died –'

'I know all about the *Jean Baptiste*.'

'You do? Then surely you, of all men, can understand. James didn't do it for himself. This is going to be one of the great scientific expeditions of the century. There will be the half dozen leading research scientists–'

'*I don't want to hear about it!*'

'Young men and women, Pete, who have given up their jobs, even sold their homes–'

'*Shut up, Karen!* I can't stand any more.'

She giggled. 'I thought, just for a moment, that you were sorry not to be going.'

'Well, think again.'

'You know, Pete, the way you bang on, one might almost think that it was your money that had been stolen.'

Vance sighed. 'It wasn't just the money, Karen. You know that. It was what the money stood for. It meant I had reached the launch pad. I was ready for lift-off. Money to me is what rocket fuel is to a space scientist, what the firing pin is to a man with a gun. Without it I'm nothing. I'm going nowhere. I'm grounded.'

'The money's gone, Pete. A lot of it went on bills for the ship. The rest is held in trust.'

'You're a trustee! *You could get most of it back!*'

'Not a hope. There are four other trustees – James, the skipper and two lawyers. They would outvote me. I couldn't get it back even if I tried. Are you listening, Pete?'

'With one ear.' A sound had alerted him, a faint whine, still very distant.

'James and I talked about changing the name of the ship – calling it after you.'

'You really thought of that? *You must be scared.*' He was irritated to find himself so taken with the notion, already reciting the name in his head. It was crazy. 'Interpol would be very intrigued.'

'Of course we couldn't call it *Peter Vance.* We would use one of your aliases.'

A siren. Approaching fast. The heads of the two men snapped around like soldiers on parade.

'I've got to blow, Karen. We could have visitors.'

'Hold on, Pete – just for a second. Supposing I were to–'

Vance dropped the telephone. Roy had squinted at the screen and was already on the stairs. Two squad cars at least.

They took the last half-flight in a long leap and ran down the narrow passage. Roy fiddled with a key.

'Come on, man! *Come on!*' Vance growled at him. Snatching the key from him, he thrust open the door and slammed it behind them. A short alleyway with high brick walls on each side and a door at the end. Roy knocked lightly on the door and then harder. '*Bob!*' he hissed. *'For fuck's sake open up!'* He danced around like a nudist in a hailstorm, his eyes on the windows behind them. Vance put his shoulder to the door and it was starting to give way when it was opened by an old man in shabby jeans and they toppled inside.

'Thanks, Bob–'

'What's all the bloody rush?' Bob grumbled, replacing his wire-rimmed spectacles on his nose and returning to his workbench by the window. 'I thought Dolly down the road must have cut her prices.'

The two men brushed themselves down and picked their way through a jumble of power tools, sanders, drills, generating equipment, arc lights, rusty old welding sets stacked against each other at precarious angles. They pushed through a bead curtain and found themselves in the main part of the shop. To their relief they saw that it was empty save for the assistant, a young man with oily black, swept-back hair and a leather tank top, who had deserted his counter and was changing the cylinder in a portable gas stove.

They were making for the door when the old man put his head through the curtain. 'Better look sharp, lads. The coppers are going mad in that office – flying around like wasps in a jam jar.'

Roy gave him a sickly smile. 'Thanks, Bob. I got a bit behind with the VAT. I'm off to see my accountant.' With a sharp look both ways, he darted into the street, his hand thrust out behind him in a two-fingered salute.

Another time Vance would have caught him, found a quiet corner somewhere and broken the two fingers but it wasn't the moment. He waited inside the doorway. He needed a few seconds to think. He wasn't collected. His brain was whirring like a fruit machine. Was the raid on Roy's office just a drugs bust or were they after him as well? Should he take a cab to the airport or go by underground? Unless the police were half-witted they would have a plain-clothes man at half a dozen of the closest stations. And when he got to Heathrow – what then? He would have a few notes in his wallet and an airline ticket to somewhere he didn't want to go.

He held his breath. Suddenly the street had gone very quiet. Like a tree that has been full of chirruping birds and then somebody lets the cat into the garden. What had happened to that sixth sense of his? Oh, Karen, Karen ... you were my talisman, my lucky charm ... why, Karen? Why? *Why?*

There was a newsagent next door. He walked in unhurriedly and bought a sporting paper, opening it fully as he went out and engrossing himself in details of the Sandown meeting. A few sauntering paces and he found what he was looking for, a door set well back from the pavement leading to the flats upstairs. From there he would have a useful view both ways. A parked car effectively hid him from any curious eyes from across the street.

He edged forward a little until his eye was flush with the edge of the building and lowered the paper a fraction. A hundred yards or so to his left, a large white police van had pulled across the roadway. He had already taken two easy strides to his right when he stopped and reversed swiftly into his recess once more. Seventy yards away an identical vehicle was nosing across the road. Policemen were emerging from the van, passing pedestrians were being checked, car drivers questioned, boots flung open. A dog handler appeared with a purposeful-looking Alsatian straining at the leash.

At the intersections with the side streets, patrolmen on motorbikes, hideously vigilant in helmets and goggles, were rolling their throttles menacingly. They reminded him of farmers at harvest time lining the stubble, watching, waiting for the combine harvester to raze the last half acre of corn and bolt the terrified rabbits from cover.

Christ! What sort of operation was this? What had they found in Roy's office? A desk diary open at the day's appointments page with his name splashed all over it? A record of the deals the two of them had done together? And what had they discovered in the basement? Heroin? Cocaine? He wouldn't put anything past that podgy little runt. *Of all the bloody awful luck!*

He found his fingers closed tightly around his pager – like a baby with a bottle. Pull yourself together, man! *You're falling apart!* You can't call Karen. She can't help you. Not here. Not now. *Not never!*

The street was emptying fast. Cars were being diverted at the checkpoint and policemen were stretching a tape from one side to the other to seal off access. An attractive young woman with long dark hair, thigh-length boots and carrying a shoulder bag had been stopped. Probably a stripper on her way to work. She stood with hands on hips while her bag was searched. He could picture the sardonic expression, the taunt waiting on the glossy, over-painted lips, the young copper colouring as he rummaged among her skimpy undergarments. Across the street a hand reached around a half-open door and a lurid illuminated 'Model' sign was snatched from the pavement. The door slammed shut.

Two plain-clothes men were steadily working their way up the street, disappearing inside shop doors, emerging a minute later, time enough to look around quickly, show a photograph, ask the question and move on. He cursed. At the rate they were going, they would be on to him within a few minutes. The best chance was an upper floor.

He was turning to look at the buttons on the bell panel beside him when he heard the sound of a window being opened above his head. Then above the growl of a motorcycle engine came the raucous blare of a loudhailer. '*This is a police message. Residents are requested to remain inside their flats until further notice. If your doorbell rings – ignore it. Under no circumstances open the door to the street. In due course an officer will identify himself to you and will request access. In your own interests...*' But the rest of the message was lost as the patrolman moved on up the street.

Vance counted the number of cars still to come past him. Ten ... fifteen ... eighteen. The tailback was diminishing fast. Soon anyone left on the street would stand out like a cowpat at a picnic site. His eyes ran down the line and then his heart gave a jolt like a kick from a horse. *Marlin!* He would recognise that short, square figure anywhere, the balding head and the long grey sideburns, the white raincoat with the military-style epaulettes. Walking very slowly up the roadway behind the last of the cars, keeping pace with his officers who were going through the ground-floor shops like ferrets working a rabbit warren. Beside him a uniformed constable noting down door numbers. Instinctively, Vance flattened himself against the door behind him. He must make his move. But what move? There wasn't a shred of cover – not a street barrow, not a news-stand – *nothing!*

Two men were coming out of a betting shop. Marlin stopped them as they crossed the street. It was now or never. Vance folded the newspaper, put it under his arm and walked briskly up the street to his left. He braced himself for a shout from behind but no, not a sound ... not yet. It had stopped raining and a watery sun put a dull shine on the pavements. To think of Karen and lover boy larking around on that ship in the Côte d'Azur, a warm sea below them and a blue sky above.

He passed an ironmonger ... a delicatessen ... a wine merchants ... coming up on the next corner another gargoyle on a motorbike. Between two parked cars he could see the booted foot and the black leggings swinging restlessly. He had to get off the street ... *but where!* What wouldn't he give for a murky, smoke-filled basement with a stripper down to a pair of tassels and a thong. And rows of grubby old men slumped in their seats playing with their marbles. But no such luck. Just a barber's pole, Sandro's Hairdressing Salon. It would have to do. He pushed open the door. One chair only was occupied. The assistant was nearly finished for he was tidying away the blow-dryer. An older man, Sandro presumably, put down his newspaper and stood up.

Vance wrinkled his nose. A faint perfume hung on the air, sweet, oily, cloying. Bogus pine panelling on the walls, a row of globular lights hanging from the ceiling like huge overturned brandy glasses.

Sandro had a fine head of grey hair and a smile which was spoiled by a stunted smoker's tooth. He gestured to the vacant chairs. 'Whichever suits the Signore…'

Vance chose the one furthest from the window. 'I want a good shampoo, a face massage and then a haircut.'

'Very good, Signore.' Sandro's dark eyes gleamed as mentally he totted up the money. Business that day had been anything but brisk.

Vance walked over to the chair. He moved rather stiffly and rubbed the back of his neck. 'I have a touch of neuralgia. I think it will be less painful if you can wind the chair down.'

The chair was depressed a few inches. 'Is that–'

'A little more. Thank you.'

Vance eased himself carefully into the chair and waited patiently while a clean white smock was produced and tied about him. He tucked his elbows in to his sides and wedged his legs tightly together. As the spray was turned on and he leaned over the basin, he squinted to his left. The other customer, three chairs distant, a young man of no more than average height, was sitting very upright. Standing together, Vance would have dwarfed him but, seated in their chairs, the relationship had been reversed. It would take a very astute officer looking at the two of them not to be misled.

'A little more soap, Signore?'

'Please. And if you have a hot face towel...'

'For your eyes ... of course, *un momento.*'

Vance pressed the towel against his eyes and allowed his head to be pushed down gently. The warm water and Sandro's sturdy fingers kneading his scalp soothed him. There was no reason why Marlin should come in. He would leave that work to his henchmen. And they wouldn't be looking for a man with fair hair. They would be working from a three-year-old photograph, the one taken at Sydney airport. It showed him with black hair parted in the centre. He even had a matching hairpiece to cover the receding forehead. Karen had detested it. Banished him from her bed for a week.

'The Signore was not tempted to go racing today?'

'No. Racing bores me.'

'Me too. Roberto, my assistant, is a frustrated globetrotter. Jules Verne is his favourite author. Do you mind if we put the television on? There is a programme being broadcast from the south of France. I promised that he could watch it. Would it disturb you?'

'It doesn't worry me,' he lied through gritted teeth. Of course it would be from Marseille. He wanted to shout at them, order them on no account to turn on the set, but he dared not attract attention to himself. *How much more of this torture could he endure!* His eyes followed Roberto as he walked over to the set. It was like being on an operating table and watching with appalled fascination as the surgeon approaches with his scalpel.

5

Karen and James Caswell had arrived at Marseille off the London flight to be met by the lawyers acting for the estate of the original sponsor. The skipper of the *Jean Baptiste*, a burly man with a leathery tan, piercing blue eyes and a grizzled beard, joined them for a working lunch in a quiet restaurant on the edge of the town. The press had found them before they finished and there were rushed interviews and photographs before they were allowed to drive to the harbour – a heart-stopping moment as they caught their first glimpse of the ship, its giant masts towering over the yachts and launches at their moorings along the quay.

There followed introductions to the navigator, the chief officer and other key members of the crew before a meeting with the leaders of the scientific team. They had been braced for some searching questions as to the identity of the expedition's new benefactor. But everyone had seemed satisfied with the picture they had painted of a millionaire philanthropist, a recluse, with a passion for anonymity.

In the atmosphere of dazed euphoria, nobody wished to inquire too closely into events whose outcome suited them so admirably. She and James allowed themselves to be swept up in the collective enthusiasm and it was three o'clock in the afternoon before they had seen around the ship and been shown their quarters. They had neither the rig nor other necessities required for a long voyage and one of the crew had been given a list of requirements and sent into town to obtain them. For a few minutes she and James had been able to talk privately and it was not far short of four when, at last, she found herself alone.

Karen paced up and down the chartroom, occasionally stopping to stare distractedly at the maps with their plots and projections and the scattering of navigational instruments spread across the huge table. What had got into her? *Why this sense of growing panic?* Wasn't this beyond anything that she and James could have imagined? It was as if a wand had been waved and they had been granted everything that they could have hoped for.

James would have the life he had only dreamed of. He would marry her, give her children, set up his research centre in some exotic island group in the Pacific – he had talked of French Polynesia – and over the years establish a reputation to rival the great naturalists of the past. What more could she ask of life than to be the wife and consort of this man? Why then was she padding up and down like a wild animal in a cage?

Under her, she could feel the gentle heaving of the vessel in the swell. She stood still for a moment, trying to quieten her breathing, putting her hands over her ears to shut out the sounds on the deck above her head, the hurrying feet, the animated cries, the shouts of laughter, the creaking of the woodwork, trying to listen to her heart. But there was no stillness, no refuge from the tumult building inside her.

Somewhere a band was playing. She went to a porthole and rubbed the glass clear. The quayside was thronged with onlookers gathered to see the tall ship put to sea. A platform had been erected and cordoned off with streamers and bunting, and the Mayor and other dignitaries of the city corporation attired in full civic regalia could be seen toasting each other in the ratepayers' champagne. A brass band was marching up and down pursued by a small crowd of urchins. At the foot of the gangway she could see James and the skipper talking to a television crew.

The planking juddered under her. The anchor chain was on the move. Karen groaned out aloud. How could she explain herself to herself? Surely she would grow to love James? Surely it was impossible not to love someone who was going to give her everything she had always wanted? What had she ever seen in Pete? How could she have tied herself to a man who offered her no future, who had bullied her, cheated her, beaten her?

But one could not wish those years away. Pete had changed her, damaged her, left her with a slight deformity that no amount of therapy could correct. James was young and inexperienced, impatient of imperfection, challenged by it. He had sensed her weakness, probed for it and found it. He couldn't leave it alone and that frightened her.

James had bragged that he had got the better of Pete, trounced him at his own game.

'You got lucky, James. Pete was off guard. But when he catches up with us, we are going to need more than luck.'

'What do you think he will do?' James tossed a lick of hair off his eyes.

'Kill us, I expect. Swarm aboard one hot tropical night, seize us in our beds and throw us over the rail to the sharks.'

'You're not serious, Karen...' He attempted a smile but his mouth quivered like a young conscript's at the whistle of the first shell going over.

She had sighed wearily. 'No, James, I'm not serious. Murder isn't Pete's style. He will probably just break both your legs and take the buckle end of his belt to me.'

'He's a bad loser,' he muttered, almost to himself.

'He is. And I don't blame him. He wouldn't have treated me the way I have him.'

James chewed at his lip, his dark eyes flickering over her. 'It's time you faced up to things, Karen.'

'What do you mean by that?' She could feel the heat rushing to her cheeks as she braced herself.

'Pete is riled because we took all that money off him, like any businessman who has been carted, but that isn't really what is getting to him.'

'You haven't talked to him since he discovered he'd been cleaned out. I tell you! *The line was red hot!*'

'And did you tell him that he had lost you as well as his money? Did you spell it out to him?'

Karen wavered. 'Not in so many words ... it wasn't necessary.'

James smiled, slowly, patiently, infuriatingly. 'So you didn't put the fire out, Karen. You made as much impression as throwing a glass of water at a blast furnace.'

'What do you expect?'

'I think you know exactly what I expect. I have pledged myself to you, Karen – without reserve.'

'And I to you.' She fanned her hot cheeks furiously with her hand.

'*Then prove it!*'

'How?' She could feel her heart fluttering like a trapped bird throwing itself against a window pane.

'Pete doesn't really believe that you have junked him. He thinks he has only to whistle and you'll come running and cobble his life together again. I tell you, Karen, that man has an ego the size of a helium balloon.'

'What can I do to Pete that I haven't done already?' she cried. 'You and I are getting married, for God's sake! What could be more final than that?'

'Oh, come on, Karen! Don't be childish! That won't stop a man like Pete. It will just whet his appetite. Only one thing will stop him. Tell him he's finished. Tell him it's all over. *Tell him you're through with him!* Tell him I can give you what he can't. He must hear it from you. It's the only way. He won't trouble us again. *Not after that!'*

'I couldn't do that to Pete. It would humiliate him. Destroy him. I have ruined him ... and left him. Isn't that enough?'

'No. It isn't enough.'

'But James, what are you asking? You can't mean –'

'Yes, I do mean –'

'But Pete is wanted by the police! They could be after me. We should bring a hornet's nest down on our heads.'

'You are a clever girl, Karen. You'll think of a way. You must. *It's him or us!'*

A great cheer went up from the spectators. Karen climbed up the ladder to the deck to see the tricolour being hoisted to the top of the mainmast. She shaded her eyes from the sun's glare to follow the small blue figures high up in the rigging. The air seemed to shudder as the sails bellied in the wind. Gulls swooped and wheeled against a sky streaked with long, trailing clouds. The ship yawed on its ropes, impatient to be gone.

Another cheer rang out as the loudspeakers, positioned at different points on the deck, crackled into life. *'All unauthorised personnel are to disembark immediately. The vessel is about to proceed to sea.'* Yet another cheer and Karen turned to see a sturdy young woman attach the Blue Peter to the halyards and run it up the foremast.

Blue with the square white centre. Unmistakeable. Sometimes when Pete had been in one of his black moods she used to bait him with it. He would be sitting in his chair brooding and then, with a gasp like an old steam locomotive, he would raise that great head of his and catch sight of the little silver flagpole.

A bellow of fury and he would jump to his feet in pursuit of her, dodge in and out of the furniture like a wing three-quarter – he was astonishingly agile for a man of his size – and after a frantic chase, corner her in the bedroom. And they would make love the way they made war. Prodigiously. Now, as she watched it snapping and stretching at the masthead, she raised her chin in salute.

James was waving at her. The television crew had climbed to the head of the gangway. 'They want a quick word with you,' he shouted. As she passed him on the deck, he stopped her. 'Now is your chance,' he hissed at her. 'This story is going over big. Tonight it will be on every news channel. Tomorrow all the newspapers will carry it.'

'*It's madness, James!* I could be arrested before we sail.'

'*Nonsense!* There would be a riot. The Mayor wouldn't allow it. Anyway, we shall be away in a few minutes.'

'But, James–'

He put his hand on her arm. 'It's so simple. Just say that you are leaving a man who has made you miserable – manipulated you for his own ends. That you never want to set eyes on him again. You are starting out on a new life with the man you love. The press will lap it up.'

'And the police?'

'They will see that you have turned into a model citizen. They won't chase you halfway across the world.'

'And Pete?'

'He won't bother us. Go on, Karen! *Give him the heave-ho!*'

She stared after him. He was heading for the foot of the foremast. There was something furtive about the way his step quickened and his hands wrapped about him as if he was trying to conceal something beneath his squall jacket. She walked slowly towards the camera crew. God help her, she didn't know what she was going to say.

Something was wrong! The camera had been trained on her but now it tilted, looked past her, the angle of elevation rising all the time, the man with the mike craning his neck. She spun around.

*****

In his barber's chair, Vance jerked his head up, knocking the spray to the ground. For a moment he thought he had gone crazy. He had heard Karen cry out. He would know her voice anywhere. He scythed viciously with his arms, lumps of foam from his hair flying across the room.

'*Out of my way!*' he bellowed. Sandro and his assistant backed away from him, knocking their other customer, who had half-risen, back into his chair. The remote control for the television skittered over the floor. Vance staggered to his feet like a Cape buffalo recovering from a tranquillising dart. He looked around wildly. And then he heard another cry. His eyes went to the television screen.

There was Karen as large as life. *She was screaming at the top of her voice.* The picture moved and now the camera was following the line of her outstretched arm ... zooming in on Caswell ... Caswell pulling on the halyards ... hauling away like a deranged hangman at a public execution ... mouthing something at her ... his features twisted into a grimace of triumph ... a yellow flag ... no, yellow and ... yellow and red ... not that signal ... *it couldn't be that* ... the one flag Karen had never flown ... never used against him ... not in all those years.

'*Stop him!*' Vance howled at the screen, but the breeze was stiffening and the flag was racing up to the masthead as if it had wings. '*No, Karen! No! Not that!*' Now it was breaking as the wind snatched at it ... yellow and red triangles... It was as if Karen could hear him for he thought she called his name and then she was running at Caswell, the fingers of her hands spreading like claws. *'Go for him, Karen!'* Vance bellowed. *'Go for that–'*

Silence! Someone had pulled out the plug. Vance swayed to an untidy standstill. Uncomprehendingly, his eyes went to the vacant socket in the wall and then up to the blank screen. He remembered a game that he had played as a child. A party game. The old lady standing by the gramophone. Afterwards there would be tea and cakes with cream and jam, balloons to pop and crackers to pull.

Wait till the music starts, children, then dance around the room. The moment it stops, you stop. And stand perfectly still. The other children went into a jerky lope like a live puppet show, their small features contorted with the effort of preparedness. But that wasn't the way to win. The trick was to keep one eye on the spinning disc, to watch for the moment the needle was lifted.

But when the music stopped, he had been far away. He hadn't even heard the door open. He followed the length of electrical cord to where it disappeared into the man's hand.

Detective Inspector Mike Marlin looked at him with curiosity. 'Yellow and red triangles?' he asked. 'What was all that about? I looked through the window and would have walked on had it not been for all that commotion.'

'So you weren't really looking for me?'

'Of course I was looking for you. We have men posted at your last known address – in Eaton Square. But when we heard that you were meeting Roy Kerr at his office, we moved up a couple of gears.'

'His phone?'

'We have been tapping it for weeks.'

Vance moved towards him but two uniformed policemen had crowded into the doorway. He shrugged and reached for a towel from the back of a chair to wipe his face. 'You are not a sailor, I take it, Inspector?'

'No. I could never afford it. My hobby is tropical fish. I have an aquarium in the sitting room.'

'Do you enjoy seeing the little fishy faces pressed up against the glass, staring at you?'

'Yes, Mr Vance. As a matter of fact, I do.'

'If only they could talk, Inspector, those boggle eyes, they could speak of marvels. Of man with his infinite possibilities, his freedom to wander to every corner of the earth, to sail the oceans, roam the skies, to leave his footprint on the surface of the moon – and yet, here is one of his kind in his little house where three small strides from one wall will bring him up short against another?' Vance scratched his head in puzzlement. 'This fish tank to which you return every evening, Inspector Marlin, where is it ... Ponders End?'

'Wherever the tank is, Mr Vance, the room is more commodious than the one that you will be occupying.' He beckoned to one of the policemen who jangled his handcuffs in acknowledgement.

'Remind me, Mr Vance, to bring my fish to see you. They may find you and your new situation even more astonishing.'

Good Connections

Captain Edward Seymour and his bride of one day were on their honeymoon and driving to Scotland. It was a warm day and the hood of their car was down. Daphne had given up trying to keep a cloche hat on her head and the air rushing past made it difficult to hold a conversation.

'I'm looking forward to getting a few days stalking,' he almost shouted. 'I used to be a pretty useful shot but this game leg of mine may slow me down.'

He had caught a piece of shrapnel in the thigh at Loos in 1915 and had been evacuated to England. A pronounced limp, a sympathetic doctor and a quiet word in the right places saw to it that he stayed in Blighty for the rest of the war. Not that he did not do his bit for King and Country. He was proud to have sat on a tribunal sorting out the shirkers from those who had a genuine reason for claiming exemption from military service. Those who tried to dodge the column got short shrift from him.

Nothing was the same after the war. Servants cost the earth, if you could find them. Daphne's people seemed to manage but her father was a banker and had a long purse. When he was widowed, Daphne stepped into her mother's shoes and ran the house.

And what a house! There must be thirty or more bedrooms in that pile, to say nothing of the land the old man owned. He had found them a cottage on the home farm. Seymour thought it a bit of a dump but he had been careful not to show his disappointment. Her father had a hearty laugh and a bluff, easy-going manner but those small eyes set deep among the red veins missed very little.

Daphne's brother had been killed in the last weeks of the war. His mother had gone into a decline and died a year or so later. Daphne would come into the house one day. As soon as he attained his majority, he would send in his papers and leave the Army. Keep his rank, of course. Major Seymour. It had a solid ring to it.

The old boy would find him a billet in the City. Nothing too strenuous. A chance to build up his connections. It was not too early to drop a hint or two about the shooting that he would be able to offer as soon as he was running the estate.

Good connections. A good school, a good regiment and a good marriage would take you a long way up the ladder. The wrong friends or an unprofitable liaison could send you sliding down the snakes. The difference between life and the children's game was that once you were down, you usually stayed down.

His father had been dealt a very moderate hand and had done a very moderate best with it. He had an administrative job in horse racing. His wife had a little money and they had managed to buy a small house in Newmarket where Edward, an only child, was brought up. His old man had a fund of good stories and was a popular figure on the course.

A rich owner and breeder had taken an interest in Edward and helped to send him to a public school and then into a well-known infantry regiment. He still helped with the mess bills. Edward planned to distance himself from his benefactor as soon as he could afford to do so. Life was like a game of whist. As one added to one's hand, one should be ready to discard, ruthlessly if necessary.

Daphne had lost so many friends in the war. Edward did not flatter himself that she would have married him otherwise. But he had caught her when she was grieving for her brother and in low spirits. He congratulated himself on his timing. Life was all about timing. Watch, wait – *and then pounce!*

He inclined his head towards the girl, admiring the way the wind tossed her fair, shingled tresses about her head. With her button nose and Cupid's bow lips, she was pretty in a rather obvious, chocolate-box sort of way. 'Perhaps you will catch your first salmon!'

She smiled and nodded. Daphne was a countrywoman first and last. She would not want to stay overnight in London. He planned to keep his bachelor flat in Half Moon Street. If he was discreet, he saw no reason why he could not see a few of his old flames from time to time. Girls like Phoebe.

Phoebe had not come to the wedding. Of course, she was cut up. She had hoped to marry him. Her people had an old rectory just off the big road that they were taking to the north. He had telephoned from the hotel the night before. It was after dinner and Daphne had gone upstairs.

Phoebe answered the telephone. She sounded very subdued. She was sorry to have missed the wedding, she said, but she had not been well. She blew her nose. Her parents were away. Why didn't he and Daphne call in for a cup of coffee on their way? 'Would eleven o'clock suit? You can introduce me to the blushing bride.'

'What a sport you are, Phoebe! Are you sure you don't mind?'

She was trying to be brave, she said in a choking voice.

'Well done, old girl. We will see you about eleven.' He brushed his moustache lightly with the tips of his fingers.

Poor Phoebe. She had been hard hit. Like a pheasant that seems to stagger in the air as the shot rips into it, then flies on gamely, losing height with every yard. But she would not make a scene. Phoebe was made of the right stuff. She would smile through her tears and pour out the coffee.

It would do his stock with Daphne no end of good. She would suspect that he and Phoebe had been rather more than good friends. He would take her in his arms and reassure her without ever laying her misgivings quite to rest. He felt sometimes that Daphne took him a little too much for granted. Not many men of his stamp had come back from that dreadful war. She should consider herself a very fortunate young lady to have that ring on her finger.

Edward had toyed with the idea of marrying Phoebe. Her father was a very decent sort. A solicitor with an old-established practice in the county town. Her mother was rather a pet but completely unworldly. Her ambitions for her daughter were so inflated it was painful to listen to her.

Phoebe had many qualities. She was topping to look at and very jolly to be with but she and her friends could be so irritating. Occasionally he felt duty-bound to remind them that millions of lives had been sacrificed to make the world a better place while, to listen to them, one would think that there was nothing more important than dances and dresses and the next party. But they would not listen. They merely laughed and shook their curls at him and ran off.

Phoebe's family had no connections that would do him any good. If he had married her, he would have had to stay in the Army or else money-grub and endure years of servitude while he waited to fill the shoes of the men above him. He would send Phoebe a nice present when he got home. If they were very discreet, they could take up where they had left off.

Edward told Daphne of the change of plan while they packed. She straightened and stared at him with her cornflower-blue eyes. 'Darling, don't look like that,' said Edward. 'Phoebe is just an old friend, a remote cousin, one of the family really. And the house is on our way.' He kissed her. 'We won't stay long.'

Shortly before eleven o'clock, they turned off the main road and drove through winding, leafy lanes to the village. The rectory was close to the church and was approached by a short drive. The bell was tolling as they drew up in front of the stone portico.

The curtains to the large sash windows on either side were partly drawn. Nobody was about and Edward peered through the gap into the darkened dining room. 'Something dreadful has happened!' he called to his wife. 'Get back in the car! *We can't stay!*'

'What are you talking about?' Daphne was already at his side.

'Have I gone mad?' Edward had covered his eyes with his hands. 'Or is there a coffin on the table with someone inside?'

'Oh, God!' his wife whispered. 'It's Phoebe, isn't it? Edward, how *could* you!'

'What have I done?' he protested shrilly. 'How can you–'

The front door opened soundlessly and a young man in sombre clerical dress approached them. He pursed his lips and looked at them reprovingly. 'There has been a tragedy here,' he said, 'you will understand that the family is unable to receive anybody at this very sad time.'

'You mean Phoebe, don't you?' Edward pointed to the dining-room table. 'How … how did she die?'

'By her own hand,' the cleric said gravely.

'But how could she! I spoke to her only last night.' Edward caught his wife's eye and raked his fingers through his hair. 'Phoebe knew that Daphne and I were coming. We were expected.' An edge of resentment crept into his voice.

The man in grey joined his hands together. 'In that case, the police may wish to talk to you.'

'The police!' expostulated Edward. 'What have they got to do with it?'

'They have just left.'

'Well, why didn't they take her with them?' he protested. 'Instead of leaving her there for–'

'Edward! Please!' Daphne took his arm. 'This is a place of mourning.'

'If you will forgive me, I will leave you to your reflections,' murmured their companion as he returned to his melancholy duties.

A moment later, a light tapping seemed to come from the house. *'Oh, Lord! They must be nailing down the coffin lid!'* Edward hurried back to the car. Daphne walked more slowly, her head down, deep in thought.

They drove away at some speed, the wheels of the car scattering gravel across the neatly tended lawn. Back at the house, eight pairs of eyes watched the car disappear.

Then came an outburst of laughter and mutual congratulation. 'Phoebe, you were marvellous,' said someone, 'and using the chest from the tack room was an inspiration!'

'I still think she should have had a short length of rope trailing from her neck,' one of the girls giggled.

The clergyman was modest about his performance. He had borrowed a waistcoat and a detachable collar from the dressing room and worn them back to front. The effect, he conceded, was very passable.

Tomorrow Never Come !

Dirk had not got the fare to London. He curled up in a ball in a corner of the compartment listening to the train rattling through the darkness, hurrying him away from everything he had known, sensing the sparks of light from beyond the windows flitting across his face like fireflies, harbingers of a brilliance that had come to him only in his dreams.

The rhythm of the wheels comforted him, the wheels that every second were taking him further away from the wet streets, the grey houses with their blank, incurious stare, the rubble-strewn alleys, the streams choked with effluent, the desolate factories and the nettle-strewn wasteland with its chain-link fences and squat, rusty gasometer.

'Tickets please!'

Dirk turned his head but made no other movement. Perhaps it was the long, livid scar among the black stubble or the way his hand was thrust inside his coat, for the conductor paused only for a moment and then moved on.

He pulled up his collar, burrowed back inside the threadbare garment and closed his eyes once more, trying to efface the images that shuttled through his head but then gave up. Let them come. The garage with its black, oil-caked floor, the inspection pit like an open grave, the machinery pressing down on his head, the cold metal that smelled like blood. The street militia, the obscenities so endemic that they formed a parallel language, the girls, coarse and predatory. Acts of extraordinary violence, the only transfiguring moments.

The face of Brad, his elder brother, when they pulled him from the canal, white and bloated like some foul fungus. The clubs with their revolving lights, the smoke, the press of bodies and the noise. Oblivion in tablet form, a nicker a time. He would never go back. Nothing could make him.

He and Brad were doing alright until the heavies started taking an interest. Make a little space for yourself, turn your face towards the sun and there they are, leaning over you like a slag heap. Big men. Big men with big boots. When you are on the ground and those boots are inches from your eyes, they look mountainous. The last thing you saw was the twin moons mirrored in the toecaps. Then came the pain.

It was safer in prison as long as you knew your place. He had played in a band for a time but he never lasted for very long. Too restless. He got a job in a travelling library. That didn't last either. *'Your job, Dirk, is to sort out the books the customers have ordered, not to skulk in the back of the van reading them.'* He had never read anything before but he went through that stuff like a rat in a dustbin. Devoured it. Looking for something he never found.

That something was still there. A nimbus that danced ahead of him, jinking out of reach like a hunted hare the moment he got close. And he did get close. A sports car that he broke into and hurtled around in for a whole day. That was something like it. But the next time it happened, it did not feel the same. It was a shock when Mum and Dad chucked him out. But a relief too. They had reclaimed their territory. He was stuck where he belonged. In No Man's Land. At last, he slept.

It was just getting light when the train pulled into the station. He got out with his battered suitcase. There was no one on the barrier but that did not surprise him. It was Easter Saturday. The day that everything in his life was going to change.

He had £6.66 in his pockets. It was all that he had in the world after he had paid his debts. He had even hocked his guitar. He walked towards the brightest part of the sky. The park was closed but he scrambled over a gate. He bathed in the fountain, stripping off his clothes and immersing himself wholly in the clear, cold pool.

He had a pang of self-doubt before he threw his money into the water for good luck. The coins glinted in the early morning light as they rolled away. He ran up and down until he was dry and then opened his case and took out the silver suit. It was covered in mother-of-pearl sequins, each one a clouded mirror. There were epaulettes on the shoulders and a high collar which fastened at the neck.

It had never been worn. The lad who had ordered it was a drummer in a band. He died from an overdose and the tailor sold it for a few pounds. Dirk dressed carefully. His old clothes and the suitcase were dumped in a litter bin. Like a snake, he had sloughed his skin. But he kept his knife.

In the distance a bell was tolling. Dirk followed the sound until he came to a large square and mounted a broad flight of steps that led to an arched entrance. The service was already underway. Shafts of sunlight in rainbow colours slanted down from stained-glass windows. The very air seemed to shake with the reverberations of the organ.

Then a priest in a golden robe stepped up into the pulpit. His hair was white like wool. His eyes were fixed on Dirk. It was as if the man could see right into his soul. 'There appeared a great wonder in heaven,' he began, 'a woman clothed with the sun and the moon under her feet and upon her head a crown of twelve stars.'

Dirk ran from the church. He ran all the way to the river and across a bridge, and threw himself down upon the grass and slept. After what seemed like hours later, he was awakened by the sound of a dragon's breath. He could feel its heat. He expected to find the monster standing over him.

A few yards away, an enormous silver balloon had landed and was about to take off again. The pilot shouted to him to come over. A small crowd had collected and they started cheering as soon as they saw Dirk. The pilot explained that he needed a little help. An American and his wife had paid for a trip over London. The guide who was to accompany them and point out the sights had not arrived. Would he stand in for him?

Dirk had never been to London before but he agreed without a second's thought. They all climbed into the basket, the guy ropes were loosened and the balloon rose swiftly into the air. A hamper was opened and a bottle of champagne uncorked. They were on honeymoon, the Americans told him. They seemed to have eyes only for each other and his duties were not onerous.

When Dirk stepped out of the balloon, the street lamps were coming on. Drawn by a glow in the darkening sky, he walked quickly and soon found himself in a square lit by huge illuminated hoardings. The pulsating neon after the champagne made him feel dizzy.

A large crowd had formed a semicircle in front of a cinema, leaving a roped-off passage in its midst. Shiny black cars were arriving and chauffeurs were jumping out to open doors. The passengers, men in dinner jackets and women in exotic evening dresses, were making their way down a red carpet which led to the entrance.

'Make way for the gentleman, if you please!' The concierge had seen Dirk in the crush of spectators and, pushing his way through them, took his arm and led him into the foyer. There was clapping and cheering and nudging and whispered attempts to put a name to this particular celebrity.

A champagne flute was pushed into his hand. He moved from one group to another. If he attracted some puzzled looks, he did not notice them. Suddenly, in the street, the hubbub was stilled and from the onlookers there came a deep sigh like a warm wind. Hero had arrived.

An open-top Bentley drew up outside. From it stepped a figure such as Dirk had never seen and never hoped to see again. A vision in fire and ice. Her hair, the colour of wheat before the sun has burnished it, was crowned with a diadem powdered with diamonds. These caught the colours of the night and sent back streams of crimson, green and gold. A glimpse of a white robe, a silver girdle, shoes which shone like glass and she was past him, smiling, stretching out her arms to those who wished her well, a queen among her subjects.

Dirk was shown to a seat. Hero was two rows in front of him. He paid no attention to the celluloid heroine. He had eyes only for the real one, so utterly captivated was he. Afterwards, he followed the luminaries of the cinema world to a line of stretched limousines and was whisked off to the reception.

On the journey, a cameraman who had drunk rather too much was holding forth. 'Hero may have been right to leave Magnox Films and go independent. Her contract was up and she didn't need them anymore. She has beauty, charm and charisma. In two words, she is box office! But it was brave, my friends, or foolhardy. It hit the company hard and their boss is not one to take it lying down.'

'Surely nobody would try to harm Hero?' someone ventured.

'I wish I could believe that,' the cameraman retorted.

'Your trouble,' said another, 'is that you have a weakness for melodrama. But we are not going to let that spoil our evening. *Lighten up, guys, we are going to a party!*'

The director of the film that they had watched was giving a buffet supper in his house in north London. As the security gates swung open to admit them, Dirk felt a tremor of nerves. The house was like a palace. It was floodlit from one end to the other.

The cars were crunching through thick gravel and stopping in front of a pillared portico. The guests were emerging and forming a line that led from the driveway to a hall lit by a magnificent chandelier. He could hear the names being announced in portentous tones.

If he joined the queue, exposure was inevitable. He would be thrown out in disgrace. He might even be arrested. He would be shaken awake in the middle of a beautiful dream and never be able to recapture it. Inside his suit, he could feel the sweat running down his arms.

His companions were greeting some friends and he profited from this momentary distraction to slip away. Somebody called after him but a border provided him with some cover and creeping along a wall, he found a door that opened into the main garden.

The smell of smoke. Dirk froze. He pinpointed a red glow in the shadows as someone drew on a cigarette. As his eyes became accustomed to the darkness, he could make out two burly shapes.

'A few guards can't cover a place this size,' one muttered.

'Let's just pray nothing goes wrong,' came the reply. The two shapes moved away.

It was a warm evening and people were beginning to come through the French windows. They had plates of food in their hands and sat at tables arranged along the terrace. Waiters busied themselves pouring out wine. Somewhere a band was playing.

Dirk looked about him. The lighting from the house spilled out over a large lawn bounded by a fence. Through the trellis, he could see lights reflected in the water. A swimming pool. To his right, a long wall hid the road from him.

A thin beam from a torch ran along the top of the wall for no more than a few seconds before leaving that area in darkness again. Dirk moved silently to the wall.

The branch of a tree gave him an extra foot of height and he looked over.

Two men dressed as waiters were at the back of a car. One of them opened the boot, pulled out a length of rope and coiled it around his waist. 'Tape?' said one of them. The other nodded. 'Cuffs?' Dirk heard the clink of metal. 'Dope?' The other patted his pocket. The boot was closed softly.

A twig under Dirk's feet snapped with a noise like a rifle shot. He ran down the length of wall and did not stop until he reached the high trellis fence. *Had the men seen him?* Dressed as he was, it seemed impossible not to have been spotted.

No sooner had he got his breath back than he saw Hero crossing the lawn. She was in a gold lamé trouser suit. The man with her wore a white tuxedo with a red bow tie. He was tanned and smiling. As Dirk watched, he took her arm and twirled her around in the first steps of a dance.

A spasm of hatred ran through Dirk like a high-voltage charge. A waiter approached the pair carrying a silver tray. Was it one of the men he had seen? Should he rush up to Hero and warn her? Her hand was already stretching out to take a glass.

Dirk was haring towards her before he realised that he had made the decision. *'Don't touch that!'* he cried. *'It's doped!'* With a scything movement of his arm, he swept the glasses onto the lawn and ran on.

There was a moment of astonished silence followed by laughter. 'Obviously drunk,' said someone. 'Or mad,' said another. 'Or both,' said a third, to more merriment.

Dirk came to a halt in the shadow of the wall. Hero's companion had moved away from the main party and was conferring with a group of heavily built men. They must be the security guards. The group broke up and the men started moving back towards the house, fanning out as they did so.

Dirk doubled back down the wall, following the line of the trellis until he came to a wrought-iron archway covered in creeper. No sooner had he gone through this and felt the paving of the swimming pool surround under his feet than he knew that he was being followed.

The pool was rectangular in shape and was lit by lanterns widely spaced along its length. At the end was a high diving board which could be reached by a tall iron ladder. Dirk took off his shoes and pushed them under the low shrubs that grew along the line of the fence.

He ran to the end of the pool and crouched down behind the ladder. Two men dressed as waiters came through the archway. They switched on their torches and separated. One moved quickly down the line of shrubs. The other searched the changing rooms on the other side.

Dirk darted into the nearest of these, keeping the door ajar to give him enough light to see inside. A shower, a few towels, a row of dressing gowns – not enough cover to hide a rat. The footsteps came closer. Doors were being opened and quietly closed. If he stayed there, he was done for.

He waited until the man entered the hut next to him and then slipped out and sidled around the corner into a small triangle of shadow. He would have to try the fence. He placed a foot on one of the slats. As soon as he put some weight on it, it creaked and started to split.

Dirk turned. They were on to him. One of them grabbed him by the arm. He swung him around and broke free. He got as far as the diving board when they caught him again, pinned him against the ladder and taped his mouth.

He started to climb. It was a bad mistake. They were helping him, pushing him up. Then one of them put a noose around his neck, paying out the rope as he moved higher. 'Loop it round a rung' said the other. They only had to let him fall to hang him.

Dirk kicked backwards and was rewarded with a curse. At the top, his legs were seized and tied together. Someone pushed him hard in the back. He toppled forward onto the diving board and plucked at the rope around his neck. It was pulled taut. He panicked, groped for the knife strapped to his calf and rolled over the edge of the board.

Dirk went into the water with a huge splash. The first time he came up he saw people running towards the pool. *'Help!'* he screamed. Even to his own ears it was just a desperate gargling sound. Down he went again. He ripped the tape from his mouth. *'I can't swim!'* he squawked as his head broke the surface.

There were people everywhere, rows of shiny white faces like plates on a dresser. Were they all going to stand and watch him drown? He pulled at the rope as he sank once more but there was no answering tug.

His legs were like dead weights. His silver suit felt as heavy as if it had been tailored from chain mail. He flapped his arms feebly but his eyes remained wide open as he passed down from one green, translucent chamber to the next.

A commotion in the water, a glimpse of something gold and he felt his shoulders grasped and his body propelled powerfully upwards. Hero, paddling along on her back, pulled him to the shallow end to the accompaniment of cheering and clapping.

'Did I nearly drown?' Dirk spluttered.

'No,' replied the girl, not unkindly.

'Then, I want to stand up but my legs are tied together.'

Hero removed the rope from around his neck, untied him and put an arm around his shoulders to support him.

'Those two men–'

'Don't worry about them. The police have got them. Now, I suggest that we get you checked over and into dry clothes and fed, and then you can tell me who you are and what you are doing here.'

Dirk fingered the burn on his neck. 'I don't want to get out just yet. In fact, I never want to get out.'

Hero laughed. 'Well, we can't stay here talking all night. I'm getting cold.'

'You mean to send me away, don't you?'

'I'm just a guest here. We all have to go home when the party ends.'

'The party never really ends – not for a star like you.'

She laughed again. 'Even a star needs her beauty sleep.'

'I'm never going home. I haven't got a home. I haven't got a name. Don't ask me who I was yesterday because I don't want to remember.'

'I would like to thank the man who risked his life for me tonight. How can I do that if he hasn't got a name?'

'This is the day that I was going to turn into someone else.'

'And have you?'

'No. I wanted to be someone so different that the person I was yesterday wouldn't recognise him if he was as close to him as you are to me now.'

'In my job I have to be lots of different people but I don't think I could do that.'

'You don't need to.'

'And you do?'

'If I am to go on living, I must. Let today end like that and you will have thanked me more than you can ever know.'

'Have you any other talents? Apart from saving damsels in distress?'

'I play the guitar. I play rather well.'

'Well, Mister No Name, we will fix you up with a bed for tonight and you can talk to my agent in the morning.'

'I don't believe you. You are just saying that to get rid of me.'

'It's true. Don't you believe anyone?'

'No!'

'Not even me?'

'Not even you!'

'You have to hope that things will get better. One cannot live without hope.'

'Hoping is much too painful.'

'So, what do you believe in?'

'I only believe in today.'

'Even a day like today must come to an end.'

Somewhere a church clock was chiming midnight. Dirk, his eyes shut tight, listened intently until the last note had faded into the darkness. He opened his eyes and turned to Hero wonderingly, 'Are you still here?'

She laughed again. 'Did you expect me to disappear into a puff of smoke?'

'Yes!'

'Well, Mr No Name, I promise–'

'No!' he exclaimed. 'You must *not* make promises!'

'Tomorrow–'

'There you go again! You are just making things worse!'

Hero stamped a foot in exasperation. 'I don't know what to say or do. *You really are the most graceless creature!'*

Dirk took her hand. 'Just tell me it is still today,' he whispered. 'Is that so much to ask?'

Artistic Licence

They found themselves in adjoining seats on a night flight from New York. He was amused by the mixed messages that he was picking up from her. Her hair was dark brown and cut rather short. The horn-rimmed glasses made her look like a schoolteacher but the matching coat and skirt in oatmeal had career girl written all over it. Her figure was nice, too, but the body language was discouraging.

She was irritated. It had been a long day and she wanted to read for a bit and then get some sleep. The guy was almost too good-looking. He would probably try to chat her up. She hated being ungracious but sometimes a girl had little choice. How long would he resist? She started counting under her breath.

As the Boeing picked up speed and the nose lifted off the runway, they reached into their briefcases and pulled out the same book. They both laughed.

He held out his hand. 'Fabio Roselli.'

'Lynn Lofgren.'

'What takes you to Italy, Lynn?'

She was a New Yorker, she said, but her mother was Italian and she had always regarded the country as her second home. 'I shall spend a couple of days in Rome and then board the train to Florence.' She was going to work for Falcone's, the fine-art consultants. 'And you?'

He was going to Florence too. He had just got his PhD, he told her. 'I want to get my doctorate and then join one of the big auction houses.' He would specialise in the European Old Masters, build a reputation and, one day, he hoped to have his own consultancy.

'So you have it all worked out. Where are you staying?'

'With Oskar Gregori.'

Lynn whistled softly. 'The Grand Vizier himself. I would like to meet him one day.'

'Perhaps it can be arranged.'

She opened her book. 'We shall see.'

***

Oskar Gregori had the nose of a Roman emperor. His face was brown and wrinkled like a Brazil nut and his forehead was broad and high and burnished by fifty summers.

Perched on a stony hillside dotted with olive trees stood his villa, filled with treasures. This morning, like every morning, he rose early, donned a white towelled robe and padded down to the swimming pool where he completed ten leisurely lengths in a style all his own.

At eight o'clock, Nella, his maid, would arrive on her bicycle carrying bread warm from the oven, freshly squeezed orange juice and, for his buttonhole, a red carnation on which the night's dew still rested. He took breakfast on the terrace and he never ceased to delight in the sweep of river far below and the sea of flame-coloured roofs from which arose domes and spires, towers and battlements under a cloudless sky.

The noise and bustle of the town as it drifted up was no more than a murmur. It was a measure of how far he had travelled from the teeming slums and fetid alleyways a thousand miles away, where humankind lived no better than the scrawny chickens that scratched for grains among the dust. He raised a coffee cup to his lips and inhaled deeply as if purging his nostrils of unwelcome memories.

After breakfast he went to his dressing room. Today was a rather special day and he dressed with more than usual care, selecting a cream silk shirt and a midnight-blue linen suit with a matching tie. His tailor came to the villa once a month. On his last visit, he had been so imprudent as to plume himself on winning a new patron, the President, no less.

'Discrimination is one thing, Ettore, imitation quite another,' he was reminded.

'How true, Maestro, how true,' acknowledged the tailor, rather crestfallen. Gregori's lips stretched in a thin smile at the recollection.

He descended to the hall. Tiled in marble, it was cool and airy, and a sculpture by Benedetto da Maiano drew the eye. In the drawing room, over the huge hearth, was a Crivelli miniature that cost a Contessa from Verona a few tears before she agreed to part with it. There were more tears to come when he secured an attribution to the great master of the school of Padua and its value multiplied tenfold.

Alessandra Di Varollo was a pretty woman but inclined to be wayward. A romantic adventure, if it is not to invite discovery and attract retribution, must be contrived as carefully as a general plans his battles. The lady had been left an exquisite miniature which he had long coveted. It eventually found its way into his hands at a *prix d'ami*, although nothing else about the transaction was so friendly. Alessandra spent an afternoon each week in the arms of a handsome waiter.

Gregori had spies everywhere. It was his business to know such things. Had she refused to accommodate him, he might not have been able to prevent report of her liaison reaching the ears of her husband. He was a nobleman of the old school and things would have turned out badly for her.

Gregori gave splendid parties. When the champagne had done its work, it was not unusual for some girl to challenge him. 'Oskar, why is it you never married?' He would turn the question with a laugh. As a connoisseur of beauty, how could he have confined himself to one woman? 'Though she were Aphrodite herself, I would have strayed. Pray, do not ask me in what direction.' He would raise the lady's hand to his lips and the message in his eyes would leave his interrogator in no doubt.

By nine o'clock, he had usually opened his mail but today he simply picked up a letter from his desk and walked through the French windows to a corner of the garden where the branches of a bougainvillea swayed gently in the light airs and from the mouth of a gorgon's head droplets of cool spring water fell into a deep stone trough.

Some weeks earlier, he had received a letter from a young man, Fabio Roselli by name, which had given him much pleasure. Fabio wrote that he lived with his mother, a widow, in Naples. She had contributed generously towards the cost of her son's studies in America at no small sacrifice for she was by no means well off.

He had recently completed a PhD in the history of art and had included his curriculum vitae. Gregori ran his eye down the page. The institutions that he had attended, widely held to be pre-eminent in their field, received a sniff of qualified approval. The professors, who had been charged with the young man's education, were not, he conceded, wholly ignorant.

Fabio planned to take lodgings in the town for the summer months before embarking on his doctorate. He would employ his time in visiting churches and galleries and steeping himself in the masterpieces of the Quattrocento. The Maestro's publications on the period, he said, were as Holy Writ to him. They would be like the pole star to a mariner as he set out on a voyage of discovery. As he prepared to hoist sail and cast off, would the Maestro do him the great honour of sparing him a few moments of his time?

It was a very seductive letter. Gregori lingered over some of the phrases: 'Guide and mentor ... keeper of the flame ... the trinity of high culture, academic prowess and intellectual rigour...' Like a healing balm, it helped to draw the sting from all the slights, the whispered calumnies that were the inevitable concomitant of celebrity.

The cheeky fellow had enclosed a snapshot. A frank, open face, a boyish smile; a white open-neck shirt that contrasted nicely with the deep-gold tan; white ducks and deck shoes which hinted at a nature not averse to occasional *divertissements* to soften the austerities of scholarship.

Fabio arrived on the stroke of noon. He was everything that Gregori could have hoped for. After a light lunch on the terrace, he was offered a month at the villa. His host would send a car for his things.

Gregori cut short the boy's thanks. 'You will live as my guest and you will live well. You will be introduced to people whom it would take you, left to your own devices, a lifetime to meet. You will learn – because what few wits I have,' he raised a deprecating hand, 'are at your service – but,' he pushed his glass aside and leaned across the table, 'be assured, you will earn your keep.'

Fabio settled into a very pleasant routine. His natural charm and Gregori's name opened all doors to him. He had the use of a Fiat and made private visits to palaces and great houses, to galleries and learned institutions. He met curators and archivists, historians and wealthy collectors. For an hour every evening, his patron would discuss the past day and plan the next.

At drinks and dinner parties, his role, Gregori told him, was to circulate among the guests and keep his ears open. Someone might have agreed to purchase a work of art subject to authentication. Another might be in temporary financial difficulties and wish to raise money on a picture or sell it quietly. 'These people do not always come to me with their troubles. They need a little coaxing, Fabio, a listening ear. Adroit advocacy is all I ask.'

Fabio met Lynn Lofgren for lunch on one occasion. They chose a small restaurant away from the centre but they were seen and the news got back to Gregori. He was very displeased. 'Keep away from that girl, Fabio. She works for Falcone's. They are competitors. I only use them when I have to.'

One morning after breakfast, a few days before Fabio's stay at the villa was due to end, Gregori took his protégé into the library. 'Fabio,' he began, 'I admit to feeling a little disappointed in you. I had hoped that you might have produced a little more in the way of results.'

He waved away the young man's protestations. 'As men grow old, they become impatient. You must not hold it against me. When I was young, I did not have your advantages. Diffidence and sensitivity were luxuries that I could not afford. I was like a plantation worker in a sugar-cane field. Everything stood in my way. I had to carve out my life with a machete.'

'It must have been hard.'

'It was hard.' He walked over to a bookcase, unlocked a drawer and extracted a large envelope. 'You have heard of Principessa Paola?' He added the name of an old Florentine family.

'Of course.'

'Then you will know that she is respected – loved would not be too strong a term for her work among the poor people of this region. You may be aware that she was recently widowed but few know the circumstances. Her husband, most unfortunately, was in the middle of renewing his life insurance when he died. The documents were not signed and he was not covered when he died.'

'He was reputed to be very rich. I assumed–'

'Assume nothing, my young friend. You will discover that reputation and reality are two very different things. I have the scars to prove it.'

'Surely he had investments?'

'They have been sold. They realised very little. He was poorly advised. Paola lives in a charming house but it does not belong to her and the lease expires in a few years. She now finds herself very short of money and, as if that were not distressing enough, her daughter is in hospital and facing a very expensive operation to save her sight.'

Fabio shook his head, 'She must be terribly worried. Is there some way that she can be helped?'

Gregori opened the envelope, slid out the contents and placed them on the table between them. 'The only asset of any value that Paola possesses is a Lorenzo Rustici.' He passed a photograph to his companion.

'It is a pleasant picture but it is small and appears to be unsigned.'

'Correct. As it stands, she would be lucky to get fifty thousand dollars.'

'You were right to call in Falcone's.'

'How did you–' Gregori's eyes darted to the flap of the envelope where the name of the firm was just discernible. His mouth worked furiously but he quickly regained his composure.

'I wanted to help Paola so, with her permission, and at my expense, I sent the picture to a fine-art consultancy where they have all the latest equipment. Falcone's produced a computer enhancement.'

Fabio turned the sheet over and held it under the light. 'It has been signed by Rustici. The signature has been effaced, probably by over-cleaning.'

'Go on.'

'If the signature has been authenticated–'

'It has.'

'Rustici was a minor figure. His name would, perhaps, add twenty-five thousand dollars to the value.'

Gregori inclined his head. 'Well done. You are a most promising pupil. We are, I think, agreed.'

'Did you ask Falcone's to produce a radiograph?'

'I did. They telephoned this morning. It adds nothing to what we already know.'

'Do you wish to purchase the picture yourself?'

'I intend to make an offer for it.'

'Is that being fair to the Princess? Surely an auction is the way to get the best price.'

'It is the best way to ensure that Paola's miseries are bandied about in the gossip columns for the next six months. The sale must take place privately and quietly – and yet we must ensure that she is not the loser.'

'I do not see–'

'How it can be done? As yet, you have not heard my terms. To help the lady, I am prepared to pay one hundred thousand dollars. It is much more than she could hope to obtain on the open market.'

'It is most of generous of you.'

Gregori shrugged. 'Money is not everything in life. I too have known bad times. Here is a chance for me to help someone who has done so much for others. But someone must bring Paola the good tidings.' Amused, he looked at Fabio and widened his eyes. 'I have an envoy in mind.'

'I will go if you wish.'

'I do wish it. I am entrusting you with an important mission and a delicate one. Paola is a proud woman. I do not want her to feel that she is in receipt of charity. Tell her of my admiration for her. Hint, if you like, at stronger feelings concealed from her out of deep respect. Take the envelope. Tell her about the signature. Make a little more of it if you wish but do not let her slip into fantasies about coming into great riches. Stress the fact that Rustici is, as you say, a minor figure. Offer her a hundred thousand dollars. Obtain her agreement to sell.'

'In writing?'

'Certainly not. She is a woman of her word.'

'She may want more time.'

'Believe me, she has no more time. She needs that money now.'

'She may wish to take advice.'

'She will take your advice.' Gregori glanced at his watch. 'It is half-past nine. She is expecting you at eleven o'clock. I have to attend a prize-giving at midday followed by luncheon.' He picked up the telephone and waited for Fabio to leave the room before dialling a number.

***

Fabio returned to his room and put on a white linen suit. From his window he saw the chauffeur hold open the door of the shiny black Mercedes for Gregori to step inside.

As soon as he heard the sound of the engine fade, he got the Fiat out of the garage. Nella came to the front door. 'The Signore will be early for his meeting.'

'The Signore has one or two things to do in the town,' he replied, forcing a smile. Infernal busybody. He drove down the hill, found a public telephone kiosk and called Lynn.

She was very upset. 'Your Lord and Master rang my CEO a few minutes ago and bawled him out for putting our name on the back of an envelope. He said it was a breach of security and that he wouldn't deal with us again. Strictly speaking, he was right but it seems very unfair.'

'He can be very unfair.' In a few words, Fabio told her about his appointment with Princess Paola. 'Lynn, I want to make sure that she is not swindled over this picture. Have you seen that radiograph?'

'Of course.'

'Can you see another painting underneath?'

'I'm not sure that I should answer that.'

'Then you have answered it. What have you said in your report?'

'There isn't going to be a report. Gregori cancelled it.'

'Lynn, I'm begging you. I must see that radiograph before I meet the Princess.'

'I will need written authority from Gregori.'

'I am his agent. Isn't that enough?'

'No.'

'I will take full responsibility.'

'That won't help me when I find myself on the street.'

'Is that your last word?'

'Fabio … there is a picture underneath. There is no doubt in my mind who painted it.'

'Don't tell me. You believe it is a–' He named one of the great masters of the Quattrocento.

'That's right.'

'I suspected it. There are two other fully authenticated examples of his pictures being overpainted by Rustici. The man was a bit of a firebrand – he made a lot of enemies and for a few years it was dangerous to own his pictures. You must let me see that radiograph, get that report typed up and send me a copy. I don't mind paying for it.'

Lynn and Fabio met in a café. Half an hour later, Fabio left for his appointment with the Princess, the radiograph securely stowed in his briefcase.

***

The school had fostered the talents of many generations of budding artists. It was the last day of term and the hall was packed with students and their relatives. Whispering among the audience had created a feverish atmosphere and the principal's overlong speech was received impatiently and rewarded with no more than polite applause.

While Gregori was being introduced, the murmuring grew and when he stepped forward to the rostrum to present the prizes, he was greeted with acclamation. There was frenzied clapping and cheering and shouts of *'Maestro!'* and it was several minutes before order was restored.

Gregori pulled an embroidered silk handkerchief from his top pocket and wiped away a tear. The gesture was unfamiliar to him but he could not remember when he had been so moved.

He had been mistaken in believing that he had reached the peak of his profession. Up to that moment, he had been standing on a false summit. The honours and decorations that had come his way were the flag that showed proof of his ascent. But today he had reached the very top. He had won a place in the affections of those to whom the torch would pass. It was deeply gratifying.

The prize-giving passed in a blur of smiling faces. One after another, the students stepped up to the platform like subjects bringing tributes to their monarch. After lunch, the principal rose to his feet, hitched his gown higher on his shoulders and spoke from hastily prepared notes.

'They say that bad news travels fast but, my friends and colleagues, good news travels faster. We learned this morning, some of us from the local radio, others from the midday paper or in other ways, that we were shortly to entertain in our midst a Good Samaritan indeed.' There was a burst of applause and it was some moments before he was able to continue.

'You will know of whom I speak when I say that a certain noblewoman, renowned for her charitable works, has been brought low by cruel blows of fate and now finds herself in need of the same generosity and support with which her name has been so long identified.'

Small beads of perspiration appeared on Gregori's brow but he resisted the urge to reach for his handkerchief. The rest of the principal's speech came to him but intermittently. He might have been standing in a diving suit fathoms deep and listening to reverberations far above him.

'The noblewoman had a picture ... selling it well was her only hope of rescue ... our Samaritan could have bought it for a certain sum ... nobody would have blamed him ... but he was determined not merely to help her ... but to deliver her. He commissioned an examination of the picture ... experts discover another underneath ... a masterpiece, no less ... worth five times as much … and that is what our noblewoman will receive…

***

Fabio returned to the villa to find that his packing had been done for him and his suitcases were in the hall. He went out into the garden and found Gregori walking slowly down the avenue of cypresses.

There was a hint of autumn in the air and the Master held the ends of a shawl to his throat. 'You do not really believe that I, Oskar Gregori, am going to pay five hundred thousand dollars for that picture, do you?' His face was as cold and grey as if it had been carved out of stone.

'I think you will. Carefully restored, it will be worth at least four hundred thousand.'

'I will be down a hundred thousand. What about that?'

'Think of it as punitive damages?'

Gregori stopped and stared at Fabio. 'How so?'

'Does the name Cristina Roselli mean anything to you?'

'Your mother?' Gregori turned back towards the house. 'I do dimly remember the name. An attractive woman. Her husband … your father … was very ill.'

'He died.'

'I am sorry.'

'He had a good job. His death left her very short of money. She had a nice picture. School of Giovanni Battista Piranesi. It was the only thing in the house that was worth selling.'

'I believe I may have bought it.' Gregori scratched his forehead. 'I recall paying quite a lot of money for it. The details will be in my ledger.'

'I remember the details quite clearly. The picture was bought unsigned. Shortly afterwards you … discovered a signature … a month later you sold it for five times what you paid.'

Gregori shrugged. 'I was lucky. Your mother could have paid an expert to examine it.'

'She could not afford it. She put herself in your hands.'

'I had no contractual obligation to her.'

'You had a moral obligation.'

'I had an obligation to the artist. I had an obligation to Art. They took precedence over my obligation to your mother. The profit was a minor consideration.'

'A profit for you but years of hardship and anxiety for my mother and her family. Is that a minor consideration?'

'To your mother, no. To me, frankly, yes. People who want a pleasing pattern of colours to put in a gold frame and hang on their walls should go to a market stall and buy one of the daubs. They should not own a great work of art because they do not know how to look at it or how to unlock its secrets. They do not know how, in the highest sense, to love it.'

'So you revenge yourself on people when they are at their most vulnerable, like the Princess and my mother?'

'It ill becomes you to reproach me on that score, you who have been treated as I would my own son and then stabbed me in the back.' Gregori pushed back a cuff and consulted his watch. 'Your taxi will be here in a few minutes. Forgive me if I do not shake hands.'

Drawing the Badger

I want to write it all down while I can still remember it. I may hide it away for years and years before I look at it again. Or, perhaps, I will burn it as soon as I come to the end.

It started at half-term. Mother asked the Badger, my housemaster, to stay for the weekend. I couldn't believe it when she said that he would be driving me home in that awful old Wolseley. We left an hour before the rest of the chaps. He thought I would be impressed but it meant that everyone saw us go. Grierson and Fraser were leaning out of the windows jeering, but the Badger pretended not to notice.

I was furious with Mother for not asking me first but she said that I was nearly seventeen and must stop being so self-centred and start thinking about others for a change. We had another of our rows. She said it was too late to put him off and, anyway, Edmund Brockett, that's the Badger, had all sorts of qualities which I would appreciate as I got older and that he was one of the few people she would like to know better.

Mother never stopped to consider what the boys in the house would say when they found out that the Badger was spending two nights under our roof. He was the butt of half the jokes in the school. Father would have understood how I felt. Popularity at school is like snakes and ladders. Climbing a ladder takes ages but you can slide down a snake in seconds.

Mother is so unworldly. She is shy and awkward and never meets anyone new. It isn't really her fault. She and Father married before the war when he was working for a forestry company. The house was isolated, which didn't worry him because he was a bit of a lone wolf, but she was on her own too much.

Father joined up at the beginning of the war and Mother rented an old vicarage near Henley. When he was invalided out of the Army, he didn't want to see anyone and she didn't have much of a life stuck in the house looking after him. I told everyone at school that he had been wounded and awarded a medal but someone asked their father if it was true. He was a general and could have given me away but he wrote and said that I was quite right to be proud of my father but I must be careful not to make up stories.

Mother said that the cold and the damp of a winter in Holland had got into Father's lungs. We could not afford to heat the house properly and he never seemed to be able to get warm and spent most of the day in a chair in the parlour in front of the fire. Sometimes I hoped he would die so that she could marry again but only if she married someone important like a war hero or a racing driver.

I didn't think things could get any worse but they did. After he died, we moved into a cottage at the end of a muddy track. I had just gone to boarding school. Boys are such snobs – always out to prove that whatever you have got, they've got something better. When anyone asked where I lived, I said that we had a farm with rough shooting and a trout stream. In fact, there was a patch of bramble where the rabbits used to run in and out and a muddy pond, but that was all.

Mother sold my father's shotgun and his stamp collection. They would have come to me but she got rid of them just the same. She never asked me if she could.

She says that I argue all the time and it just makes her tired. Then, in the next breath, she says things like, 'John, you are the head of the family now, so we must make the big decisions together.'

Mother went to see the Bursar, Mr Hudson, to tell him that she would have to take me away from the school because she could not afford the fees. I was not supposed to know in case it unsettled me. As if I could have been more unsettled than I was already.

They came to some sort of arrangement about the fees and Mr Hudson started to think of himself as part of our family and asked me to tea once a month to find out how I was getting on. You couldn't keep that sort of thing quiet – or perhaps Mr Hudson couldn't – because it was all round the school within days that I was a pauper and living on the school's handouts. Fraser took to carrying coins in a tin box and shaking it whenever I went past as if he was getting up a collection for me.

I was in Lupton's house for two years before he retired and the Badger took over his house. Lupton had the best house in the school. We won the cricket cup and the football cup three years running. He never missed an important match. Once, when I was captain of the junior rugger team, we got into the County Schools Final. He knew I was nervous and he grabbed me as I was going onto the pitch. 'What are you going to do today, Dawkins?' he asked in that fierce way that he had.

'Win, Sir,' I said.

'Win!' he bellowed. *'Of course you are going to win!* What else are you going to do?'

'Beat them hollow,' I replied.

'That's more like it!' he said. 'Now go out and give them such a drubbing they never come back!' And he gave me a great clap on the back and I charged onto the field like a fighting bull and we won twenty-four to fifteen.

The Badger wasn't interested in winning. He didn't really like games. He said they pandered to our tribal instincts. In one of my reports he wrote to my mother and said it was his dearest hope that when the boys left his stewardship, it would be as perfect gentle knights equipped for life's tourney. Mother loves that sort of thing. Within a year, all the cups had gone.

The house started to rot from inside. The prefects had no authority. The rest of us competed to see who could break the most rules. Chaps went to the cinema or race meetings or disguised themselves and took the train to London to visit the nightclubs.

Half-term was dreadful. Whenever I was with them, Mother and the Badger talked about me – my grades, my chances of getting to university, my career. But somehow it all seemed a bit phoney. Then it came to me. They weren't really interested in any of that. This was their way of getting closer to each other. I was a sort of alibi.

Mother really admired him. If you saw the Badger on the football pitch, with his pebble glasses and black hair parted down the middle, beep-beeping on that absurd whistle, you would know how ridiculous he looked. Ridiculous to you but terrifying for me.

In the last month of the term, the Badger asked Mother to tea with his two unmarried sisters, Maud and Enid. In the house we called them Arsenic and Old Lace. They were pale, anaemic creatures who seemed to spend all their time knitting socks or reading Victorian novels.

Mother told me that the two old bats stood up after tea and said that they had an announcement to make. They had decided to buy a small house in Eastbourne. The Badger cried and they hugged him and said there, there, they were in a bit of a groove and the sea air would do them good.

Mother said it was rather noble of them and that they probably did not want to go but they must have been anxious in case they were holding Edmund back. *Back from what!* Things were moving too fast.

The Badger said that he wanted to change the curtains in the private wing and asked Mother's advice about fabrics and colours. Mrs Lindsay, our matron, picked up on this very quickly. She came to my bedroom just before lights out and I could tell that she was upset. Angry and sad at the same time.

Your mother is a dear person, she said, but she wasn't quite sure what her plans were. Could I give her any guidance? I was fond of Matron but I didn't dare show my hand. I was as mystified as she was, I told her. She said that the Badger wanted her to move out of the private wing at the end of the term. She was worried about what sort of rooms she would be given.

Her husband died of something dreadful before they could have any children. When she was in a good mood, she said that we were her children. She had a small flat with a bathroom right underneath the Badger's bedroom. She liked taking her bath late when the water had heated up again but she could never relax because the Badger slept badly and he paced up and down for hours at a time.

I sucked up to Mr Hudson when I went to tea. I told him that I was worried about the lack of discipline in the Badger's house. There was an illegal telephone system, I said, which ran between the boys' rooms. Of course I did not tell him that Norton brought it back from Hong Kong and that it did not work most of the time.

I put on my most solemn expression and said that I was worried about the effect that it was having on our work.

'I'm glad you told me, dear boy,' he said, and put his arm around my shoulders and we went into the garden. 'Strictly between ourselves, Dawkins,' he added, 'Mr Brockett has had two warnings from the headmaster.'

The next day, an electrical contractor arrived and put ladders up against the house and spent the morning disentangling the wiring from its hiding places among the ivy and the gutters. The Badger called Sneath, the head of house, to his study and asked him what he knew about the telephone system.

Half an hour later, the jungle drums were beating. The Badger was very agitated and kept clicking and flicking his double-jointed fingers. 'These infractions of school regulations have got to stop and stop at once,' he said. 'Boys are smoking and drinking and going up to nightclubs in London. There is going to be a cleaning of the Augean stables.' When his back was to the wall, the Badger always dragged in a classical allusion or a Latin tag. It probably comforted him to think that even heroes, like Hercules, got themselves into a mess from time to time.

Sneath was only head of house because he was clever. He had already got a scholarship to Oxford and had no interest in keeping discipline. He couldn't provide the Badger with a list of the villains because he genuinely didn't know who they were. The best that he could do was to say that the roof of the house was where most of the smoking and drinking went on.

The next day was a Saturday. After games, we had tea and then the smokers and drinkers amongst us would normally carry our contraband up the stairs to the attic where there was a door to the roof. We had our parties in the valley gutter between the two slopes because we couldn't be seen from the street.

Of course none of us went up there that evening. Mrs Lindsay tipped off Bevan Major that the Badger was planning to pounce and the grapevine did the rest. Just before six o'clock, I heard someone padding along the corridor. I looked through the keyhole and saw the Badger, dressed as for school in his suit and gown but wearing thick mauve football stockings on his feet.

I waited until he reached the door to the attic and then crept after him. I got to the top of the stairs just as he reached the door to the roof. He left the door on the catch and pulled it to behind him. I released the catch very quietly. Poor old Badger was locked out on the roof.

Within a minute or so, he started banging on the outside door. I shut the door to the attic and listened hard but I couldn't hear him. Then I rounded up half the house and we went to the tuck shop across the street. The sky was full of dark clouds and the rain was pelting down and blowing quite hard, and we sat at tables by the window in the dry, munching flapjacks and waiting.

The Badger must have climbed up the roof because he suddenly appeared on the top. He was waving frantically and with his gown swirling about him he looked like a great big black crow. Suddenly he lost his balance and had to clutch at the tiles to avoid sliding down the slope.

Somehow he managed to pull himself up to the top of the roof. As soon as the rain eased off, we moved outside onto the pavement, partly to get a better view and partly because some of us were preparing to rescue him if he seemed to be in real danger. Then the headmaster's wife, Mrs Simpson, who was passing in her Morris, stopped to find out what was going on.

That was a mistake because a tile landed on the roof of her car and she jumped out and looked up, and saw poor old Badger thrashing about in his mauve stockings. She grabbed Sneath and marched him over to the house and the rest of us followed in a disjointed crocodile.

We never heard about the rescue because Sneath was forbidden to talk about it. After prayers, the Badger read a poem called 'Invictus', which is quite solemn but Bateman spoilt the effect by hiding a cuckoo clock under the table. It squawked *'Cuckoo!'* at the end of each verse and had us all in stitches.

On the Sunday, I had to go and have tea with Mr Hudson. He told me, in strict confidence, that Mr Brockett's future was under active consideration. 'He is not a well man, Dawkins,' he said. 'You boys could do a lot more to support him.'

On Monday morning, I got an awful letter from Mother. The Badger had telephoned to ask her advice. He was considering resigning for the sake of his boys.

She said that he was suffering from great perturbation of spirit. She never says things like that so she must have got it from him. He was like a wounded animal, she said, who had been hunted and harried until he didn't know which way to turn.

He needed a real home, she said, not that bear pit of a house. Most of all, he needed the love of a good woman. That really shook me. She ended with an appeal to my better nature, which I hadn't got, at least not at the time. She said that she had only had half a marriage and I shouldn't blame her for wanting the other half.

I lay awake all that night. Mother wasn't in love with the Badger. That was impossible. Nobody could love the Badger. But she pitied him so much that it came to the same thing. If I didn't do something drastic, she would marry him and live in the private wing and bring him home in the holidays. The Badger would be my stepfather. Nobody would ever speak to me again.

I was so desperate that I couldn't think properly. Then I got the idea in carpentry. It just came to me. It was the wildest idea I had ever had. On Wednesday there was the annual confirmation service. The house would be empty between eleven and twelve. I bought a jar of mustard pickles and rubbed it into my face and told Mrs Lindsay that I felt ill.

She said I looked frightful and sent me to bed. When everyone was in church, I bundled up my sheets and went to Mrs Lindsay's bathroom and spread them over the bath and the floor. Then I went up to the Badger's bedroom with the drill I had nicked in the carpentry class.

I drilled a hole through the floorboards in a dark corner of the Badger's bedroom. Then I looked through the hole. The sawdust had fallen straight down onto the towel that I had put over the bath. I threw the drill onto the top of the Badger's wardrobe and went down to the bathroom again. I picked up the sheets and scooped up the sawdust. Then I returned to the Badger's bedroom and arranged the sawdust in a little ring around the hole.

It was just after midnight when Mrs Lindsay screamed. She was sitting in her bath and the Badger was pacing up and down as usual. Then he noticed that there was a tiny beam of light in the corner of his room so he went over to investigate. That's when the sawdust fell on Mrs Lindsay.

She jumped out of the bath and grabbed a towel, turned off the light and shone a torch at the ceiling. She found the hole straight away and there was the Badger's glassy eyeball staring straight at her. That's when she screamed.

That was the end for the Badger. He appealed to the governors but the drill had been discovered by that time and there was no reprieve. He didn't try to put the blame on us, which was jolly decent of him. It was the first time I felt sorry for him.

On the last day of term, after evening prayers, he asked us to sit down. He got to his feet and this is what he said, or as much of it as I can remember.

'By now, all of you know that I shall not be your housemaster next term. I am going to take a long holiday. The school has very generously offered to keep a teaching post open for me but it is too early to decide about things like that.

'It is almost too late … but, mercifully, not quite too late … to say how acutely I feel that I have let all of you down. The truth is that I know nothing about boys. For all my years as a teacher, I have had this idealized picture of *the schoolboy*. It has encased me like a suit of armour and my vocation has been to fit out each of you, plate by plate and rivet by rivet, until you are as close to this image as I can make you.

'I have failed, and failed abysmally, as I deserved to. The craftsman, whether in wood or stone, in glass or metal, does not lift his hand to begin his work until he has acknowledged the primacy of his material, allowed it to speak to him, learned its ambitions so that he can foster its strengths and mitigate its weaknesses.

'I had in my hands the most precious … and sometimes … the most intractable of materials ... but in my arrogance and stupidity, I have neglected to follow the craftsman's example. If I had married and had a wife and children to love me…'

The Badger stopped talking and I swayed back in my chair and hid in case he was looking at me. Then he went on, 'If I had had a wife or children to love me and tease me out of these silly notions, things might have been different – but it was not to be. You have taken your revenge but I consider that I have escaped lightly. I shall not be as easy upon myself.'

Henderson Minor started to blub and Jenkins kicked him. We all went home the next day. A week later, at breakfast, Mother showed me an article in the newspaper. It was no more than a few lines. It was headed *Schoolmaster Lost at Sea*. It said that Mr Edmund Brockett, a housemaster – it gave the name of the school – had planned a holiday in France and had taken a ferry from Dover, but he was not on the boat when it docked at Calais. It was greatly feared that he had fallen overboard.

Mother stared at me and I stared back at her until we began to frighten each other, but we didn't say anything.

In Brief

Charles Owen writes the Army obituaries for the Daily Telegraph. He has been variously a stockbroker, a merchant banker, a cavalry officer, a Ministry of Defence contractor and an engineering export salesman. *Cry Cassandra*! and *Fiamma* were published recently. Four collections of short stories – *A Crack in the Glass, The Mark of the Beast, Man Overboard* and *Escapade* – are now being published simultaneously.

Meet the Author, Charles Owen

I was born in 1935. When the Second World War broke out a few years later, I was shipped off from a Devonshire hill farm to Australia. My father, who was wounded in the First World War, was then in MI5. He believed that the Germans might invade and probably wanted my mother, sister and myself out of the way.

In 1942, we were returning to England when we were torpedoed by a German submarine in the North Atlantic. The ship was sent to the bottom but after taking to the waves in a lifeboat we were all rescued by the US Navy.

Aged 12, I went to Eton. Top hats were being phased out. They were routinely maltreated until the boys wearing them looked like something out of the music hall. But if the school was slowly changing, the house where I boarded lacked all mod cons and was later pulled down.

In 1956, in my first term at Cambridge and despite the objections of the Foreign Office, I set off to Budapest in the hope of helping the Hungarians in their revolution against the Soviets. My involvement made little difference to the outcome of that tragic affair but the experience provided the inspiration for my forthcoming book, *The Dido Decrypt.*

I did my National Service with a cavalry regiment in Germany. Our job was to discourage the Red Army from crossing the Rhine. As a tank commander, it was wise to keep well in with your driver. If he was cross with you, he would give you a bumpy ride which would loosen every tooth in your head.

A spell in stock-broking and merchant banking persuaded me that I was better at making things than making money and there followed many productive years as the export director of an engineering company. We were contractors to the Ministry of Defence and there was a lot of travelling to the Middle East. The work was absorbing, exacting and, sometimes, frightening.

In 2000, for the Daily Telegraph, I began writing up the stories of the surviving men and women who had been awarded the Victoria Cross or the George Cross. That led to writing the obituaries of those who had had adventurous and distinguished careers in the British Army. To date, several hundred of these can be read on the internet.

In the course of reading private papers and unpublished memoirs that have passed through my hands, I became fascinated by the exciting and often perilous careers of servicemen and women who were involved in Intelligence operations; spies and counter-spies, secret agents and members of the Special Operations Executive who were parachuted into enemy-occupied countries to train and arm the Resistance. *The Voce Vendetta*, relating the fictional exploits of Captain Rohan Voce, will be published in 2016 and will, I hope, bring an account of some of these clandestine operations to a wider readership.

Acknowledgements

My heartfelt thanks go to Georgie, my daughter, who helped to unravel the seemingly impenetrable mysteries of the word processor, also to my son, Jamie, whose guidance has proved invaluable in my wanderings through the trackless wastes of journalism; and to Pierre, my brother-in-law, whose expertise, unstintingly shared, kept my spirits up and my blood pressure down when the hardware and software sulked or threatened to mutiny. I have nothing but praise for the unwinking editorial eyes of the proof-readers. Rosie, heroically volunteered to give the manuscript a final vetting. Any errors that remain are my responsibility.

www.ingramcontent.com/pod-product-compliance
Lightning Source LLC
Chambersburg PA
CBHW031335060726
47590CB00007B/2471